S.CREAM SHOP

Day of the Dead

P9-DEL-054

By Tracey West

For Kathy, Patrick, Ellen, Helen, Sandi, and DR, who helped me celebrate Day of the Dead for the very first time, and taught me how to live la vida loca—T.W.

For my grandmother Ruby Hall Dow, who introduced me to the wonders that lay within the secret garden of my imagination—B.D.

If you purchased this book without a cover, you should be aware that this book is stolen property. It was reported as "unsold and destroyed" to the publisher, and neither the author nor the publisher has received any payment for this "stripped book."

The scanning, uploading, and distribution of this book via the Internet or via any other means without the permission of the publisher is illegal and punishable by law. Please purchase only electronic editions and do not participate in or encourage electronic piracy of copyrighted materials. Your support of the author's rights is appreciated.

Copyright © 2004 by Tracey West. Illustrations copyright © 2004 by Brian W. Dow. All rights reserved. Published by Grosset & Dunlap, a division of Penguin Young Readers Group, 345 Hudson Street, New York, New York 10014. GROSSET & DUNLAP is a trademark of Penguin Group (USA) Inc. Printed in the U.S.A.

Library of Congress Cataloging-in-Publication Data is available.

ISBN 0-448-43360-5   10 9 8 7 6 5 4 3 2 1

S.CREAM SHOP

PICK YOUR PATH

Day of the Dead

By Tracey West
Illustrated by Brian W. Dow

Grosset & Dunlap • New York

"I can't believe we're going to miss Halloween," Hector Ramirez grumbled. He kicked a small stone with his sneaker and watched it roll off the sidewalk and bounce on the street.

Hector's twin sister, Eva, walked beside him. "Stop complaining, Hector," she said in that sometimes prim voice of hers. Even though Eva was only older than Hector by twenty-three minutes, he had noticed that lately she liked to act like she was *ages* older than he was.

"But this is probably the last time we'll get to go trick-or-treating," Hector said. "We're twelve already."

"So?" Eva shrugged.

"So!" Hector was indignant. "No Choco-Bites. No Fruit Rocks. No Sugar Sticks. It's not fair!"

"You can buy those in the store any day," Eva pointed out.

Hector kicked another stone. "It's not the same," he mumbled. It was no use arguing with Eva. It never was.

"Besides," Eva continued, not realizing the argument was over. "There'll be lots of amazing things to eat at Tia Rosa's in Mexico. Tamales, empanadas . . ."

"But no candy," Hector interrupted.

"Well, there are sugar skulls," Eva said. "But most people don't actually eat them. They're mostly pure sugar."

Hector licked his lips. "I'll take a dozen, then."

Eva shook her head. "Too much sugar is bad for you, Hector," she said, sounding exactly like their mother.

Hector didn't reply, and the twins walked in silence as they made their way to downtown Bleaktown. Their mom had sent them to find a present to give to Tia Rosa when they arrived in Mexico.

Hector thought about the trip they were taking tomorrow, and felt that familiar nervous sensation creep into his bones. A lot of things made Hector nervous, although he would never, ever admit that to Eva. Flying on a plane made him nervous. And it didn't help that they were going to Mexico to celebrate el Dia de los Muertos—the Day of the Dead.

Tia Rosa had sent them a bunch of books so they could learn about the holiday, held in Mexico from October 31 to November 2. On those days, people remembered loved ones and ancestors who had died by creating altars called *ofrendas* in their homes. The *ofrendas* were deco-rated with flowers, pictures of people who had died, and images of skeletons and skulls.

That's what made Hector nervous. In the pictures in the books, the grinning faces of skeletons were everywhere—in streets, storefronts, and homes.

"That seems like a strange way to honor your ancestors," Hector had said at the supper table the day the books had arrived.

"I think it's beautiful," said Hector's mother. "People believe that the spirits of the ancestors return to Earth on the days of the dead. The skeleton faces are there to make them feel welcome."

"The skulls also make the living aware of their own mortality," Mr. Ramirez added. "By staring death in the face, you don't have to be afraid of it."

That did not make any sense to Hector at all. If he ever came face to face with a skeleton, he'd turn around and run away. He wouldn't stay and make friends with it.

There was another part of the festival that Hector was nervous about, too. In many parts of Mexico, people took flowers and food for the ancestors to the graveyard and held a picnic there. One picture Hector saw showed two kids spreading out a blanket next to a brightly painted tombstone. The graveyard had looked colorful, but it was still a graveyard. Hector didn't even like to ride past one in the car. Thinking of the rows and rows of dead people always made him shiver.

But they were flying out tomorrow, and there was no way Hector could get out of it. Maybe it wouldn't be so bad. At least the sugar skulls sounded good.

"I think we should go to the gift shop on Main Street to find Tia Rosa's present," Eva said, breaking the silence. "Maybe we could get her a picture frame."

"Whatever," Hector said. It didn't matter, anyway. Eva would pick out what she wanted, no matter what Hector thought.

The twins turned down Wary Lane. Even though it was still afternoon, the sun was already sinking over the tops of the trees. A shaft of orange sunlight struck the window in a store across the street, glinting on something inside.

Hector squinted and stopped, curious. The other items in the window were unusual—old suitcases, peacock feathers, a Chinese vase, a violin —so what was doing all that gleaming? Hector stepped off the curb and walked across the street.

"Hey! That's not the way to the gift shop," Eva said, annoyed, but she followed him across.

Hector walked up to the window and saw that the gleaming object was, of all things, a skull. Not a real skull; it was made of some kind of silver and was about as big as an apple. The skull had hollow eyes and a mouth of grinning teeth.

"Maybe Tia Rosa would like it," Hector found himself saying. "She could put it on her *ofrenda* for the Day of the Dead."

Eva frowned. "I don't know," she said. "I think they use special skulls for the Day of the Dead."

"The book said that they make skulls out of all different materials, whatever they can find," Hector said, feeling proud that he had remembered something Eva hadn't. "So what's the difference if Tia Rosa gets it from us?"

Eva looked up at the sign above the store, which read: "Sebastian Cream's Junk Shop."

"I don't think it's polite to get somebody a present from a junk shop," she said.

"We don't have to tell anyone where we got it," Hector said, surprising himself. He had been letting Eva have her way since he was about five years old. It was just easier that way. But for some reason, he really wanted to get the skull for Tia Rosa. "Come on. Let's go in."

Eva sighed and followed him inside the shop. The walls and floors were crammed with shelves, and each shelf was crammed with objects of all kinds. In the very back of the store was an old wooden counter and cash register. And behind the cash register was the strangest looking man Hector had ever seen.

The man was so short that his head barely reached above the counter. He had a round face and body, and a round ring of white hair around his bald head. He looked at the twins through a pair of round, wire-rimmed glasses.

"Good day," he said. "I am Sebastian Cream. How may I help you?"

"The skull in the window," Hector blurted out. "We're going to visit our Tia Rosa in Mexico. We want to get it for a present."

Mr. Cream's green eyes twinkled behind his glasses. "Ah, el Dia de los Muertos," he said, nodding. "That would be a lovely gift for someone celebrating the Day of the Dead."

Hector glanced at Eva, who seemed impressed by Mr. Cream's comment. But she would not let go of her stubbornness.

"We only have fifteen dollars," she said.

"That should be enough," Mr. Cream said. He came out from behind the counter and walked toward the window display. Then he stopped suddenly and put a finger to his chin thoughtfully.

"Then again, I may have something else that might interest you," he said. He turned on his heel and walked to a display case across the room. Hector and Eva followed him. One shelf held all kinds of brightly painted wooden animals. In the very center of the display were two skeleton figures standing on a green base. The whole sculpture was about as tall as a pencil. Both figures wore colorful hats. One figure was playing a guitar, and the other held a maraca in each hand.

Mr. Cream gingerly lifted the skeletons off the shelf and held it out to Eva and Hector.

"It's a *calaca*," Eva said.

Mr. Cream nodded. "That's right. Skeleton figures that are made out of papier-mâché and are dressed or decorated to represent people from all walks of life. This one is quite nice. It shows two mariachi players, you see. Musicians."

"I like it," Eva said, reaching out a finger to carefully touch it.

"It's nice," Hector said. "But I like the skull better."

If the twins purchase the silver skull for Tia Rosa, go to page 12.

If the twins purchase the *calaca*, go to page 16.

Continued from page 11

"Come on, Eva," Hector said. "You always get to decide everything. I saw the skull first. We wouldn't even have come into the store if it wasn't for me."

"I guess," Eva relented. She hated to admit it, but her brother had a point.

"So it's the skull, then," said Mr. Cream. Without waiting for an answer, he walked back to the window display and removed the skull. He brought the skull to the counter and started writing up a bill. The skull's hollow eyes seemed to be staring right at Hector, and for a split second he wondered if he had made the right choice.

Then Mr. Cream carefully wrapped up the skull in tissue paper and placed it in a bag.

"Enjoy your trip to Mexico," he said, handing the bag to Hector. "I'm sure you will find it quite interesting."

The shop owner's voice had suddenly taken on a curious tone, Hector thought, and he felt the urge to get out of the store as quickly as he could. He felt better when he and Eva were back outside on the sidewalk.

"It's good that we're done early, anyway," Eva said. "I'll have more time to pack."

Hector shook his head. Last night, he had thrown some shirts and jeans and socks and underwear into his bag and shut it. Packed. No problem. But for some reason, Eva was taking days to do the same thing. Sometimes he wondered if they were twins at all, they were so different.

Hector and Eva went home. Hector did some homework; as he studied, he could hear Eva pulling out all of the clothes in her closet in her bedroom next door. Then Mrs. Ramirez came home from her job at the library.

"We're having pizza for supper tonight," Mrs. Ramirez said. "I'll be too busy packing to cook."

Well, that explains where Eva gets it from, Hector thought. His mom ordered the pizza—half plain, half pepperoni, with breadsticks on the side—and then turned to Hector and Eva.

"So did you find a nice present for Tia Rosa?" she asked.

"Hector picked it out," Eva said quickly, as though she knew her mom might object to the skull.

"Let's see it," Mrs. Ramirez said.

Hector unwrapped the skull and set it on the kitchen table. His mother nodded and smiled.

"So you've been paying attention to our talks about el Dia de los Muertos," she said. "Good for you! Tia Rosa will love it."

"What's Tia Rosa like, anyway?" Hector asked. He didn't know anyone else who had an aunt who liked skulls.

"Tia Rosa is your abuela's youngest sister," she said. "She and your grandmother were a lot alike."

Hector had never met his grandmother, who had died in Mexico when he and Eva were just babies. But his mother had always told stories about how much she had loved music and dancing. She sounded like a lot of fun.

Hector's father came home a few minutes later, and he admired the skull, too.

"Just perfect," he said. "I'm glad to see you both are getting into the spirit of things."

"I don't know about Hector," Eva said. "He told me he doesn't even want to go!"

"I just said I didn't want to miss Halloween," Hector shot back, "not that I didn't want to go."

"Stop it, you two," Mrs. Ramirez warned. Then the doorbell rang.

Hector's mother went to answer the door, and Hector sat down on a chair next to the skull.

Then he gasped.

The skull's eyes were gleaming, as though light was coming from within. Hector had reached over to pick up the skull when he heard a crash. He ran out to the front hall.

A huge wind had kicked up outside, causing the open front door to quickly swing back. It knocked into the pizza delivery guy, who tumbled down the stairs. The pizza flew out of his hands, soared across the room, and landed with a thud as the box hit the floor by Hector's feet.

The pizza guy wasn't hurt, but the pizza was too smushed to eat. Mrs. Ramirez paid for it anyway, and Mr. Ramirez went out to pick up burgers instead. In all the commotion, Hector completely forgot about the skull.

But by the time they were done eating, Hector remembered the skull's gleaming eyes. He took the skull into his room and examined it. He poked it and patted it and shook it, but he couldn't get the eyes to light up again.

Then Eva walked into his room. "What are you doing with that? We need to wrap it for Tia Rosa."

"There's something weird about this skull," Hector said. He told Eva how its eyes had gleamed right before the accident.

"Maybe it's bad luck or something," Hector said. "I think we should leave it home."

If Hector and Eva leave the skull at home, go to page 23.

If Hector and Eva take the skull with them, go to page 27.

"The *calaca* is much nicer," Eva said in a firm voice that meant Hector was not supposed to argue with her.

And, as usual, Hector gave in. "All right," he said. "We'll buy the *calaca*."

Eva beamed, and Mr. Cream nodded. "A fascinating choice," he said, which Hector thought was a rather odd thing to say.

Eva handed over the money, and Mr. Cream wrapped the *calaca* in tissue paper and placed it in a small bag. He handed it to Eva.

"I hope you enjoy your Day of the Dead celebration," he said.

"Thanks," Eva replied. "Come on, Hector."

As Eva and Hector walked home, Hector's mind wandered to the plane trip they were taking to Mexico tomorrow. The thought of flying on a plane made him just as nervous as the thought of going to a cemetery.

When they reached their house, Eva unwrapped the *calaca* and placed it on the kitchen table. "I want to show Mom and Dad," she explained.

The twins' parents came home from work about an hour later. Mrs. Ramirez carried a pizza box.

"I didn't want us to have to do any dirty dishes

the night before our trip," she said, placing the pizza on the counter. Hector's stomach growled. He could smell the pepperoni through the cardboard.

"Sounds good to me," said Mr. Ramirez, rubbing his belly. Then he noticed the *calaca* on the table. "What's this?"

"I picked it out," Eva said. "It's our present for Tia Rosa."

Mr. Ramirez picked up the *calaca*. "Ah. Mariachis. That's very nice. A mariachi is a Mexican street band. That's what they call the musicians, too."

"Tia Rosa will love it," Mrs. Ramirez said. "She and Abuela used to love to see the mariachis play at festivals."

"Tia Rosa and Abuela were sisters, right?" Eva asked.

Her mother nodded. "Yes," she said. "Tia Rosa is the youngest. They looked very much alike, those two. Although they were different in many ways."

"How different?" Hector asked.

"When they were younger, your abuela was very outgoing. A little bossy, even. Tia Rosa was quieter and not as brave," she said. Then she smiled. "Their story reminds me of you two."

"I am not bossy!" Eva protested.

Nobody bothered to disagree with her.

"Let's eat!" said Mr. Ramirez.

The family sat around the kitchen table and ate the pizza. Mrs. Ramirez, for the hundredth time that week, reminded them to be on their best behavior at Tia Rosa's. The twins promised they would be good for the hundredth time.

After supper, Eva went upstairs to finish packing. Hector had already packed earlier in the day, so he decided to finish his homework before the trip. Before he knew it, it was time for bed.

Hector must have stared at the ceiling for an hour, thinking about the plane trip. How did that big plane, with all those people, stay up in the air like that? It seemed impossible. Worried thoughts drifted across his mind until he finally fell asleep.

Hector dreamed he was flying through the air, his arms outstretched. Below him were the blinking lights of Bleaktown.

In the dream, the air suddenly became filled with the sound of music. It was a happy sound, with guitars and trumpets and shaking percussion. But the sound startled Hector, and in the dream he began to fall, and the ground below was speeding toward him . . .

Hector woke with a start. It was only a dream. Except that he could still hear the music.

It sounded like it was coming from downstairs.

Had somebody left the radio on? He knew he wouldn't be able to sleep unless he did something about it.

Hector rubbed his eyes and sleepily walked into the hallway, only to find Eva standing there.

"Do you hear it, too?" he asked.

"Somebody must have left the radio on," Eva said.

The twins walked downstairs. The radio in the living room was off.

"It sounds like it's coming from the kitchen," Hector said.

But when they walked into the kitchen, the music suddenly stopped. Moonlight shone through the kitchen window, illuminating the *calaca* on the kitchen table.

"Maybe it was coming from outside," Eva suggested.

"Maybe," Hector said. He was too tired to think about it, actually. They both climbed upstairs and went back to sleep.

The next morning was a frenzy of packing as the family got ready for their early flight. Eva remembered to pack up the *calaca* just in time.

Hours later, sitting in Tia Rosa's house, Hector was surprised that he had been so worried about the plane. The flight had gone smoothly, and they had landed in Mexico City before Hector knew it. Tia Rosa had taken them sightseeing, and then back to her bright blue house in the neighborhood of Coyoacán.

Tia Rosa was a slightly plump woman with a wide smile and lots of curly gray hair. Now she was telling them all about the *ofrenda* she had set up for her sister, Marcela—the twins' grandmother.

The *ofrenda* was a table covered with a white cloth and then topped by two boxes covered in white, each smaller than the other, so that the shape of the *ofrenda* was like a wedding cake. A framed picture of a woman with gray hair sat in the center on the very top layer. "That is your abuela," Tia Rosa said.

The picture was flanked by two purple candles and two vases filled with orange flowers. "They are *cempasúchil*," Tia Rosa explained. "Marigolds. Their scent lures the spirits of the ancestors back home."

Tia Rosa showed them sugar skulls, tiny skulls molded from sugar, left to harden, and then decorated with icing and foil. "The skulls represent death, and the sugar represents the sweetness of life," she told them.

Bowls of apples and oranges filled the other layers. "The ancestors are hungry from their long journey back to the living," said Tia Rosa. "Tonight we will make tamales to add to the altar tomorrow. They were your abuela's favorite."

Hector licked his lips. "They're my favorite, too," he said.

Eva brought out the bag with the *calaca* in it and gave it to Tia Rosa. She smiled when she unwrapped the tissue paper.

"Mariachis! How wonderful!" she cried. "This is just perfect for the *ofrenda*." Then she carefully placed the *calaca* amidst the marigolds and flickering candles.

Soon it was time for bed. Tia Rosa and Hector's parents went upstairs to sleep, leaving Hector and Eva in the living room with makeshift beds of blankets and pillows. Hector fell asleep as soon as his head hit the pillow. He had no worries tonight.

That night, Hector dreamed of walking through a dark alleyway. Music played in the distance—the same music from his dream the night before.

Hector woke with a start. He was awake, but the music from his dream was still playing. He looked over at Eva's bed, and saw that she was awake, too.

"It's coming from outside," she whispered.

"How can it be the same music?" Hector wondered. "Yesterday we were in Bleaktown. Today we're in Mexico."

Eva didn't answer. She walked slowly toward the front door. Hector found himself following her. It was like the music was compelling him to go toward it.

Eva put her hand on the doorknob, then stopped.

"We should stay inside," she said. "Mom would be mad."

"I want to find out what it is," Hector said, surprising himself. He wasn't afraid at all. He just had to follow the music.

If the twins follow the music outside, go to page 45.

If the twins go back to bed, go to page 94.

"That is the most ridiculous thing I have ever heard," Eva said, shaking her head. "The skull didn't make the wind blow. I bet its eyes didn't glow, either. They were probably just reflecting light from a lamp or something."

Everything Eva said made sense, of course. But Hector still had a weird feeling about the skull.

"It wasn't a light from a lamp," Hector said firmly. "It was like the skull was alive or something. I'm not making it up. I could feel it."

Eva looked into her brother's eyes, and must have seen something there that made her change her mind, because her face softened.

"What will we do about a present?" she asked.

"I'll use my own money," Hector said quickly. "We can buy something at the airport. Then when we get back I'll take the skull to that shop and get my money back."

Eva nodded. "All right," she said. "We'll just tell Mom and Dad we forgot to pack it."

Eva left, and Hector flopped back on his bed, relieved. Then he got a strange sensation, like someone was watching him. He sat up and saw the skull on his nightstand. It seemed to be staring right at him.

"Sorry," Hector said, picking up the skull in his hand. He stuffed it under stacks of T-shirts in his bottom dresser drawer, then shut the drawer tightly. He didn't want that skull staring at him all night.

When his alarm went off the next morning, Hector wasn't thinking of the skull at all. He had something else to worry about—flying to Mexico on a plane. Since Hector was a naturally nervous person, the thought of flying on a plane gave him a lot to be nervous about. Eva, of course, wasn't nervous at all.

"Flying in a plane is safer than riding in a car or walking across the street," she repeated that morning at breakfast. "Plus, it's fun. You get to see the world from up high."

"You get free pretzels, too," Mr. Ramirez added, smiling. "And soda. It's just like going to the movies."

Sure, Hector thought. *If the movie theater was a thousand feet in the air with nothing underneath it to hold it up and speeding across the sky.*

And then the Ramirez family packed the car and hurried to the airport and waited on line for what seemed like an hour to check in. Eva pretended that they had left the skull at home by mistake. They bought a picture frame with flowers around it in the airport gift shop and the lady behind the counter wrapped it up for them. Hector put the present in the duffel bag he brought with him on the plane.

Then it was time to board the plane. Hector stuffed his duffel bag underneath the seat in front of him. Eva and Hector sat next to each other in one row. Eva took the window seat, and Hector sat in the middle, even though no one came to sit in the aisle seat. Their parents sat two rows in front. Hector read the card that told you how to escape from the plane and put on your life jacket twice, just to be sure.

The takeoff was smooth, and Hector found himself relaxing, to his surprise. In fact, he soon drifted off to sleep.

He dreamed of a blue sky with peaceful white clouds floating in it. Then, suddenly, the sky grew black and the clouds turned gray and gathered together. In his dream, the clouds formed the face of a grinning skull, and in the next moment, they turned into the silver skull. Bright green light flashed from the skull's eyes, and it flew through the air toward Hector.

Hector woke with a start. It was just a dream. But when he turned to tell Eva about it, he saw that the sky outside the plane had turned black also. The plane was rocking and moving like some giant hand had swept down from the sky and was shaking it.

"It's turbulence," Eva said. "We flew into a storm or something. But the captain says it'll be over soon."

Then the plane rocked again, and Hector lurched forward in his seat. He fell back again with a thud. Then he felt something bump into his sneaker.

Hector reached down to see what it was.

And there, grinning up at him, was the silver skull.

"Aaaaah!" shrieked Hector.

"It's just turbulence," Eva snapped. "Stop being such a baby."

"No," Hector said, pointing down. "Look!"

Eva looked down and saw the skull. "I thought you left it at home," she said.

"I did!" Hector insisted. "You must have put it there."

"I did not!" Eva protested.

The plane shook again, and the skull started to roll away.

"Better pick it up," Eva said, "before it rolls down the aisle."

"It can roll off the plane for all I care," Hector said. "I'm not touching that thing again."

If Hector lets the skull roll away, go to page 35.

If Hector picks up the skull, go to page 65.

Continued from page 15

"Hector, it's all in your head," Eva said. "There's nothing wrong with that skull. The wind made the pizza guy fall. Not the skull."

Hearing Eva say it out loud made Hector feel calmer. Of course the skull hadn't caused the accident. That was just silly. He had probably just imagined seeing its eyes glow.

"You're right," he admitted. Then Eva wrapped up the skull and stashed it in her luggage.

The next morning, Hector was too nervous about the plane flight to even think about the skull. He had never been on a plane before, and he spent all morning thinking about all the things that could go wrong.

Hector and Eva and his mom and dad headed out to the airport after breakfast. Mr. and Mrs. Ramirez sat two rows in front of the twins, who had a whole row to themselves. Hector was surprised at how smooth the takeoff was. Outside the plane, the sky was blue and the sun was shining. After a few minutes, Hector forgot all about being nervous.

Before he knew it, Hector heard the captain's voice over the speakers.

"Ladies and gentlemen, we are now approaching Benito Juarez Airport in Mexico City," he announced. "If you look out of your window, you can see the ring of volcanic mountains that circles the city." Then he repeated the announcement in Spanish.

Eva had the window seat, so Hector leaned over her to look out. He could see the tops of the white-capped mountains in the distance. Not long after, the plane began its descent.

When they got off the plane, they found themselves in a crowded airport terminal. A plump woman with a friendly smile and a curly mop of black hair streaked with gray pushed through the crowd toward them. She wore a bright pink dress.

"Tia Rosa!" Mrs. Ramirez cried. She and her aunt hugged each other. Tia Rosa gave Mr. Ramirez a hug, too. Then she turned to Hector and Eva.

"How big you are!" she said. "I haven't seen you since you were little babies."

She hugged them both tightly. Then she led them to the baggage claim area while they told her about the flight. When they got their luggage, Tia Rosa led them to her small yellow car in the parking lot. Hector and Eva squeezed in the back with their mother.

Hector got stuck in the middle—Eva always got the window when she wanted it—so he had to crane his neck to see the sights as they drove through downtown Mexico City.

"I thought we'd drive through the Zócalo on the way," Tia Rosa called to them in the backseat. "It's the historic center of Mexico City."

"Isn't it the second largest square in the world?" Eva asked.

Hector saw Tia Rosa smile brightly in the rearview mirror. "Ah, somebody has been reading the guidebook. Good girl."

Hector was annoyed with Eva for showing off, but forgot about it as soon as they entered the Zócalo.

We're definitely not in Bleaktown anymore, Hector thought. Tia Rosa's little yellow car moved slowly through the traffic—the streets were crammed with more cars than Hector had ever seen. Around them, old churches reached for the sky with tall towers and round domes. Then they passed tall office buildings. In the entryways of the buildings, Hector could see tables filled with orange flowers, candles, and white skulls.

"Here in the city, *ofrendas* are not just for homes," Tia Rosa said, noticing Hector's curiosity. "Most office buildings have them, too."

Tia Rosa turned down a street lined with shops, and Hector gasped to see skeleton faces staring back at him from every window. The window of a bakery was painted with laughing and playing skeletons. Another shop window held rows of grinning skull masks. For the first time that day, Hector remembered the silver skull in Eva's bag and its weird, gleaming eyes. But of course, that had been his imagination.

The traffic thinned out as Tia Rosa drove them to her neighborhood in Coyoacán. "Coyoacán is part of Mexico City, but it's like its own little village," Tia Rosa explained as they drove through. Hector could see what she meant. It wasn't as crowded as the city they had just seen. The cobblestone streets were lined with trees. They drove past little shops and cafés until they arrived at a pretty street with small, brightly colored houses. Tia Rosa stopped in front of a small house painted bright blue.

Inside, the first thing Hector noticed was the large *ofrenda* in the living room. The *ofrenda* was a table covered with a white cloth and then topped by two boxes covered in white, each smaller than the other, so that the shape of the *ofrenda* was like a wedding cake. A framed picture of a woman with gray hair sat in the center on the very top layer. The picture was flanked by two purple candles and two vases filled with orange flowers. The other layers were so filled that Hector could barely take in all that was there. He saw skulls, skeleton figures, apples, oranges, more orange flowers, and a glass of water.

"Wow," Hector said. The *ofrenda* didn't look scary or creepy at all. It looked, well, just special.

"Yes, it's very beautiful," Tia Rosa said. "I will tell you about it in a little while. But first, we will eat. You all must be very hungry."

Tia Rosa fed them chicken and tortillas and rice and had bottles of sweet, syrupy soda pop for Hector and Eva, which Hector thought was delicious. When they were done, Tia Rosa showed them the *ofrenda*.

"The flowers are *cempasúchil*—marigolds," she told them. "Their strong scent lures the spirits of the ancestors back home. The glass of water is to quench the spirits' thirst."

She pointed to Abuela's picture. "Our ancestor spirits return to us this one night. It is our duty to make sure they are fed and honored. In turn, they will protect us if we need them to."

Next, Tia Rosa picked up a skeleton figure. It was a *calaca*, just like the one Hector and Eva had seen in Mr. Cream's shop, except this one was dressed like a woman in a fancy dress.

"The skulls and skeletons are here to show the spirits of the dead that they are welcome," Tia Rosa explained. "They also remind those of us living that death is always near."

Hector found that the idea didn't sound so scary when Tia Rosa said it in her soothing voice.

She handed him the *calaca* and he examined it. Then he placed it back with the others—a man in a suit, a mermaid, and a doctor.

"I almost forgot," Eva said behind him. "We have a present for you, Tia Rosa."

Eva got the skull from her bag. Tia Rosa unwrapped it and smiled.

"Wonderful!" she said. "You two really are in the spirit of things. Thank you."

Tia Rosa put the skull on the altar, amid the *calacas* and orange marigolds. Hector had to admit that it looked perfect there. It didn't look scary at all.

"The *ofrenda* is almost finished," Tia Rosa said. "Tonight we will finish making tamales and empanadas to add tomorrow. Then, when the sun goes down, we will take everything to the cemetery to Abuela's grave."

Hector felt nervous all over again. He was not looking forward to the picnic in the cemetery. Then again, Tia Rosa made the whole celebration seem happy, not scary. Maybe it wouldn't be so bad.

The family spent the rest of the day helping Tia Rosa make tamales, seasoned meat wrapped in corn husks. Back home, Mrs. Ramirez only made them on special occasions. Hector couldn't wait to bite into one.

"We must wait until mañana," said Tia Rosa.

"Tomorrow we will eat."

By the time night fell, Hector was tired and not nervous at all anymore. He realized he had completely forgotten about Halloween and trick-or-treating. He hadn't missed it at all.

Tia Rosa's house was small, so she set up blankets and pillows for Hector and Eva in the living room. She turned off the lamps in the room, but left the candles on the *ofrenda* lit. Then she kissed Hector and Eva good night.

"Tomorrow will be even better than today," she promised.

Hector found himself staring at the flickering candles on the *ofrenda*. The light cast shadows across the papier-mâché skulls and *calacas*. The light gleamed off of the silver skull.

And then, just like the night before, the skull's eyes began to glow with eerie light. Hector sat up.

"Eva!" he hissed. "Look!"

"What?" Eva lifted her head from her pillows and rubbed her eyes.

"The skull," Hector said. "It's doing it again."

Eva looked at the *ofrenda*. "It's just a trick of the candlelight."

"No it's not," Hector said. He stood up and cautiously walked closer to the *ofrenda*.

Something on the *ofrenda* was moving.

Hector stopped, too afraid to move. As his eyes

adjusted to the flickering light, he saw that the little skeleton figurines were moving around. It looked like they were dancing.

Hector rubbed his eyes. He felt something brush his shoulder, and jumped. It was only Eva.

"Do you see it?" he asked.

"It has to be a trick of the light," his sister said, but she didn't sound so sure.

Then, suddenly, it all stopped. The light faded from the silver skull's eyes. The *calacas* stopped their dance.

Hector's whole body felt ice cold. He ran back into the living room and burrowed under his blanket.

"There is no way I am going to the cemetery tomorrow," he said. "This is all way too weird."

Eva shook her head. "You have too much imagination, Hector. That's your problem," she said.

But Hector knew, deep in his very bones, that it was not his imagination. There was something evil about that skull. Just plain evil.

To follow Hector, who stays home from the cemetery, go to page 42.

To follow Eva, who goes to the cemetery with her family, go to page 61.

Continued from page 26

"Don't be silly," Eva said. "You probably just put it in your luggage by mistake. We might as well give it to Tia Rosa. If you won't get it, I will."

Eva leaned across Hector's seat, but the plane shook again and the skull rolled underneath his seat. They could hear it clattering down to the back of the plane.

"I'll go get it," Eva said, starting to take off her seat belt. But Hector pointed to the lighted-up sign just above them.

"No moving around the plane," Hector said smugly. "There's turbulence, remember?"

Eva sighed and sat back. "When this is over, I'm going to get it."

But the turbulence did not end. Outside, the sky grew darker and darker.

Finally, the captain's voice rang out over the plane's loudspeaker.

"Ladies and gentlemen, we can't seem to find a way out of this storm system," he said. "We'll be making an emergency landing at the nearest airport. The crew and I are confident that we will make a safe landing, so please don't worry."

Hector knew that this was all because of the skull. The skull had been bad luck from the beginning. It was causing the storm. And now the plane was going to crash.

Hector kept his eyes closed tightly as he felt the plane surge lower, trying to get below the storm and ready to land. He gripped the armrest so tightly that his knuckles began to throb.

And then, finally, it was all over. The plane made a bumpy landing at the airport, and then leveled out.

As soon as they landed, Hector's parents came running back to their seats and wrapped them both in hugs. They rushed off the plane as soon as they could.

"Are we still going to Mexico?" Eva asked.

"I don't think so," said Mr. Ramirez. "Your mother and I were pretty shaken up after that turbulence."

"We're going to rent a car and drive back to Bleaktown," said Mrs. Ramirez.

Later, in the backseat of the rental car, Eva turned to Hector. She patted her bag.

"I got the skull when we were leaving the plane," she whispered.

"No way," Hector groaned.

"Don't worry," she said. "I don't want to keep it. Let's take it back to that junk shop and see if we can get our money back, at least."

Go to page 92.

Continued from page 81

"I *know* I'm right!" Eva insisted. "Throw the rosemary over your left shoulder."

Hector obeyed, and Eva did the same. The ghost was getting closer by the second.

"Now close your eyes and turn in a circle three times to the right," Eva instructed.

The twins closed their eyes. Eva counted out loud as they turned. "One . . . two . . . three!"

They opened their eyes.

The ghost was gone.

Hector spun around and looked behind him, just to be sure. No ghost.

"I guess you were right," he said.

"Of course," Eva replied.

The twins continued to follow the music down the street. The street ended in a dead end, but there was a vacant lot on the right, and the music seemed to be coming from there. The twins climbed the low, broken fence into the lot.

Hector got on his knees. "It's coming from underground somewhere," he said, excited.

Eva nodded. "We just need to find the exact spot!"

The twins walked around the lot until they found the spot where the music was the loudest.

"Stay here," Hector told Eva. He spotted an old, rusty shovel leaning against the fence. He ran and grabbed it.

The twins took turns digging in the ground. They didn't have to dig far when the earth began to cave in underneath the shovel, revealing some kind of pit. Hector knelt down.

It was difficult to see anything at first, but Hector could make out two shapes in the pit below.

Two skeleton shapes.

"Eva," Hector whispered. "I think we found them."

Eva knelt down beside him. Hector took the shovel and kicked dirt away from the opening even more.

They were skeletons, all right. They looked the same, except that one skeleton clutched a battered guitar in its arms, and the other held a maraca in each bony hand.

Eva gasped. "The mariachis."

As the twins watched, a soft glow came from within the skeletons. Hector saw that the glow looked like a transparent human form. The glowing forms rose up from the skeletons, floated out from the pit, and hovered in front of Hector and Eva.

Hector could not believe his eyes. The ghostly

forms did not look like skeletons. They were two identical men, with handsome faces, dark hair, and fancy suits covered in spangles and embroidery. The battered guitar that the skeleton held looked shiny and new in the hand of the ghost. The ghostly maracas were painted in bright colors.

This must be how they looked when they were alive, Hector realized.

The twin brothers smiled at Hector and Eva.

"Thank you," they said together. "Our spirits can rest now. We can join the great fiesta in the sky."

And then the ghostly figures floated upward toward the stars, until Hector and Eva could not see them anymore.

"Tia Rosa will be happy," Eva said.

"I'm happy, too," said Hector. He pulled the *calaca* of the mariachis out of his pocket. "I'm glad we bought this instead of the silver skull. It was nice to be able to help those twins."

"I told you," Eva said. "I'm always right!"

THE END

Continued from page 100

Without another word, Hector and Eva climbed out of the grave. They ran as fast as they could, climbed the fence, and tore down the street without looking back.

When they couldn't run anymore, they stopped, puffing and panting.

"Do you know where we are?" Hector asked.

"I think so," Eva said. "At least we got away from that creepy ghost." She shivered.

The twins found their way back to Tia Rosa's house a short while later. They climbed up the stairs, exhausted and dirty. Before they entered the living room, they stopped in front of the *ofrenda*. The candles were still lit, their flickering light illuminating the *calaca* of the mariachis.

"Just like the skeleton brothers," Eva said. "It's almost like we were meant to help them, isn't it?"

Hector frowned. "I guess. But we're just kids! How were we supposed to help them with that ghost after us, anyway?"

"I know," Eva said. "Still, I feel kind of bad."

Hector felt bad, too. But he also felt safe, and that felt good. Without even changing his clothes, Hector climbed into bed.

Once again, Hector dreamed. This time, he

was back in the grave of the skeleton brothers. Their bones had fallen apart again, and their skull faces looked sad perched on top of them.

Then Hector heard a cackling laugh. The evil ghost loomed over the grave, laughing. His bones shook underneath the tattered rags he wore.

Hector woke up, sweat pouring down his body. That face was so hideous, he'd never forget it. Not as long as he lived.

Hector closed his eyes and leaned his head back toward the pillow.

And then he heard the laugh.

He sat up. He wasn't dreaming this time. It was the laugh of the evil ghost. Hector turned to see Eva sitting upright, a look of terror on her face.

The evil ghost floated through the wall of the living room and hovered in front of them.

"You know my secret," he said in a cold, raspy voice. "And now you both will pay."

"Noooooooooo!" Hector and Eva screamed.

THE END

Continued from page 34

Hector didn't change his mind. The next day, Tia Rosa took them sightseeing around Mexico City. They spent the afternoon piling the finished tamales and empanadas onto plates and putting them on the *ofrenda*. But when the sun set, and it was time to go to the cemetery, Hector pretended he was sick.

"My stomach hurts," he told his mother, which was true. Just thinking about going to the cemetery tied his stomach in knots.

Mrs. Ramirez felt his head. "You do feel a little warm," she said. "Maybe I should stay here with you."

Hector suddenly felt guilty. He didn't want his mother to miss out on the cemetery, just because he was afraid of the skull.

"I'm twelve, remember?" he said. "I can stay here by myself. I'll be fine."

Mrs. Ramirez exchanged a worried look with her husband.

"We'll come back to check on him in half an hour," Mr. Ramirez promised.

Tia Rosa kissed Hector on the forehead. "Feel better," she said. "I am sorry you will not see your abuela's grave tonight. But I will tell her you send your love."

Hector felt guilty again. But then he saw the silver skull on the altar, and he knew he was doing the right thing.

He helped the family pack up the food, candles, sugar skulls, the picture of Abuela, the marigold flowers, and the silver skull to take to the cemetery to decorate Abuela's grave.

"I still think you're being silly, Hector," Eva told him as they got ready to leave.

Hector shrugged. "I'd rather be safe than sorry," he said.

By the time Hector's family set out, stars twinkled in the dark blue sky above. Hector waved good-bye as they disappeared down the street. Then he stepped into the quiet, empty house.

Hector walked past the *ofrenda*. The *calacas* were still there, and the surface was scattered with the heads of marigolds that had fallen off of their stems. But at least the silver skull was gone. Hector felt relieved to be away from it.

He went into the living room and took a book out of his duffel bag and started reading it. After a few chapters, he suddenly felt thirsty. He got up, stretched, and headed into the kitchen for a glass of water.

Hector was reaching into a cabinet for a drinking glass when he suddenly felt an ice-cold chill creep up his back. Had he left the door open? Hector turned around . . . and nearly dropped his glass.

The orange flowers were floating in the air above the *ofrenda*. Then they began to swirl around, as though picked up by the wind. But Hector could see that the door was shut, and the windows were closed. So what was making them move?

Then the flowers stopped swirling. They landed on the table. It looked like they had formed some kind of a pattern. Hector gently set down the glass on the table and took slow, cautious steps toward the *ofrenda*.

When he got close enough, he could see that the flowers had spelled out words:

HELP EVA

Hector rubbed his eyes. He had to be seeing things. A trick of the light, like Eva would say.

Eva. His sister was at the cemetery with the skull. Did she really need his help?

"It's just my imagination," Hector whispered. "I just need to get some sleep."

If Hector goes to the cemetery to help Eva, go to page 55.

If Hector decides to go to bed, go to page 89.

Continued from page 22

Hector didn't even bother to argue with Eva. He turned the knob himself and opened the door.

The music was clearer now. Hector turned to his sister, expecting her to tell him he was being silly, they should go back inside. But she didn't say anything. Her eyes held a faraway look.

Wordlessly, the twins stepped into the night and continued down the street. The music got louder as they walked. They turned a corner, then another, and found themselves in some kind of shopping district.

They came to another intersection, then stopped. The music was clearly coming from the right, from somewhere down a dark and narrow street. They looked at each other and nodded. Then they turned.

A figure was coming toward them. It moved slowly and smoothly, almost as though it were floating, Hector realized. Something deep inside Hector told him to cross the street, turn around—anything to get away from the strange figure. But the music called to him. Hector kept moving, with Eva right at his side.

Hector's heart started to pound as the figure came closer. It might have been human once, but it wasn't now. Its whole body glowed with an eerie, gray light. Tattered rags hung from its body, and as the rags swung back and forth, Hector thought he could see bones underneath.

But its face was worst of all. A sunken, hollow face, with sharp black eyes, a gaping mouth, and a jagged scar across one cheek.

For a second, Hector forgot about the music. The figure was about ten feet away now, and coming closer. They had to get away.

"Eva, snap out of it!" he yelled, shaking his sister. Eva blinked, and then a look of horror crossed her face, as though she were seeing the figure for the first time. She stifled a scream.

"Run!" Hector yelled. The twins turned around and ran back to the corner.

The figure was there, waiting for them. Hector and Eva skidded to a stop.

"What now?" Eva asked.

Behind them, Hector could hear the music, stronger than ever.

"Let's try to run for the music again," he suggested. "Maybe whoever's playing it can help us."

Eva scanned the street. "That didn't work before," she said. "There's a little alley between those stores over there. Maybe we can lose this thing if we go that way."

If the twins run into the alley, go to page 138.

If the twins run toward the music, go to page 97.

"Let's go to the marketplace, then," Hector
agreed. He was too used to letting Eva have her
way.

The twins walked off the side street onto a
more crowded street bustling with people getting
ready for the Day of the Dead celebration. They
asked for directions to the marketplace, and soon
found themselves in a small square filled with all
kinds of stalls.

Hector and Eva spoke a little Spanish, and the
vendors in the marketplace spoke a little English,
so they were able to find what they needed without too much trouble. Luckily, their parents had
given them some Mexican pesos for spending
money yesterday.

They found the last ingredient—a spike from
an agave cactus—at a stall filled with plants and
flowers.

"We just need one more thing," Eva said.
"Something to mix it all in."

Hector spotted a stand selling clay pots, and
they bought one just big enough to fit the skull.

"Where should we do it?" Hector asked.

Eva scanned the marketplace and spotted a
small bench in the corner. "Over there," she said.

They sat down and put the bowl between

them. They dumped in the bottle of orange water, then added the other ingredients. When they were done, Hector picked up the skull.

"Here goes," he said.

Hector carefully dipped the skull into the potion. Then he and Eva waited.

Eva frowned. "That Señor Grito is making a fool of us. This isn't working!"

Then, suddenly, a white puff of smoke erupted from the bowl. Hector and Eva coughed. When the smoke cleared, the bowl was empty—except for one sugar skull.

Hector picked it up. "Wow," he said.

"The potion worked," Eva said simply.

Hector grinned. "I know what I'm going to do now," he said.

Eva shook her head. "Hector!"

Hector took a bite from the sugar skull and licked his lips. "You know what they say. Revenge is sweet!"

THE END

Continued from page 64

Eva thought about Hector, who was so afraid of the silver skull that he had stayed home. All this time, she thought he had been imagining things. But he wasn't. She could see it with her own eyes.

For once, she decided maybe Hector had been right about the skull all along. She raised her arm and then hurled the skull like a baseball into the darkness of the crypt. She heard a thud, and then a crunching sound.

Eva breathed a sigh of relief. She wasn't sure what she was going to tell Tia Rosa. But somehow, being rid of the skull for good seemed worth it.

Eva stood up and took a step toward Abuela's grave.

Underneath her foot, the ground shook.

A low, rumbling sound filled the cemetery. The ground shook again, harder this time, and Eva watched oranges and apples roll off of grave beds.

In the next instant, thousands of marigold flowers flew off the graves and straight up into the air, like geysers. The petals showered down on the cemetery.

People began to run and scream in fright. The next thing Eva knew, Tia Rosa had grabbed her by the arm.

"Come, Eva," she said. "I do not know what is happening. But something has gone wrong."

As they ran toward the exit, Eva craned her neck to look back at the crypt. An eerie green glow shone from deep within.

Eva shivered and looked away.

I guess maybe I shouldn't have thrown that skull into the crypt, Eva thought.

THE END

Continued from page 72

Hector was pretty fed up with his sister. It was so obvious to him that the skull was causing all of the accidents! For once, he stood up to her.

"I'm telling Tia Rosa," he said. "I don't want anything else bad to happen."

"Fine," Eva scowled. "If you want her to think you're crazy, then go ahead."

Hector waited until his parents left the kitchen. Tia Rosa stood by the sink, drying dishes. Eva stayed behind, too. Hector knew she was waiting to see Tia Rosa laugh at him and tell him how silly he was.

"Tia Rosa, I need to talk to you," Hector said. He took a deep breath. "It's about the silver skull we brought you," he said. "I think there's something wrong with it. Ever since we got it, bad things have been happening."

To Hector's surprise, Tia Rosa nodded. "I think you are right," she said. "I got a strange feeling when I looked at that skull."

"I told Hector we shouldn't buy it," Eva said. Hector glared at his sister.

Tia Rosa looked thoughtful. "The skull has brought us bad luck. We need to make sure the bad luck goes with the skull, too. I know someone

51

who may help us. We will go in the morning."

Tia Rosa left the skull on the *ofrenda* for the night. Hector didn't sleep well because he kept expecting something else bad to happen. But the night passed peacefully. After breakfast, Tia Rosa started on a new batch of tamales. Then she asked Mr. and Mrs. Ramirez if she could take Hector and Eva out for a little while.

"I would love some special time with my niece and my nephew," she said.

"Of course," said Mrs. Ramirez, smiling. "We'll finish the tamales while you're gone."

Before they left, Tia Rosa took the skull and tucked it into her handbag. Then she led Hector and Eva through the neighborhood until they came to a narrow side street.

They turned down the street, and Hector saw an unusual shop right in the center of it. The front window was jammed with all kinds of unusual-looking objects.

Hector looked at his sister. "Does this remind you of anyplace?"

Eva nodded. "It looks just like that junk shop where we got the skull."

Tia Rosa opened the door and they stepped inside. The store was filled with shelves crowded with old books; paintings; false teeth; colorfully painted, carved, wooden animals; and hundreds of other things Hector could barely take in. In the back of the shop was a low counter, and behind the counter, sitting on a stool, was a round little man.

The man was Mexican, and the ring of hair around his head was black instead of white, but otherwise he looked very much like Sebastian Cream. He looked over the tops of his wire-rimmed glasses at them and nodded.

"I do not usually stay open on el Dia de los Muertos," said the man. "But this morning I said to myself, open the store today, Señor Grito. Someone needs you."

"You were right," said Tia Rosa. She took the silver skull out of her bag and handed it to Señor Grito. He held it up to his glasses and examined it carefully. Then he nodded toward the twins.

"Did they purchase this?" he asked.

Tia Rosa nodded.

"Then I must deal with them," he said. "That is how it must be."

"I understand," said Tia Rosa. She turned to Hector and Eva. "Señor Grito is a good man. Will you stay?"

Hector and Eva both nodded. Tia Rosa hugged them both. "Good luck," she said. "I will see you soon."

Tia Rosa left the store. Señor Grito hopped down from his stool. He walked in front of the counter and looked at both of them.

"The skull must be cleansed in a special solution," he said. "Because you two purchased the skull, you must be the ones to do it. I will give you a list of ingredients. Mix them together, then bathe the skull in the potion. The skull will cause you no more problems."

Señor Grito scribbled furiously on a piece of paper for a minute. Then he handed it to Hector and Eva. The ingredients were strange: orange water, dried red chili powder, an onyx stone, and some other things. "You must find the ingredients on your own," he explained. Then he handed them back the silver skull. "Good luck."

"Uh, thanks," Hector said. He and Eva stepped outside the shop.

"That was weird," he said. "That guy was just like Mr. Cream!"

"Maybe it's his Mexican cousin or something," Eva said. She looked at the list and frowned. "These ingredients look unusual. We drove past a marketplace yesterday. Maybe we should try there first."

If the twins decide to go to the marketplace to get the items, go to page 47.

If the twins decide to look for the items back at Tia Rosa's house, go to page 141.

Continued from page 44

Hector closed his eyes and opened them again. The flowers seemed to stare back at him, silently shouting their message: $HELP$ EVA.

Hector knew what he had to do. If Eva was in trouble, he had to help her. She was his twin sister, after all.

Finding the cemetery wasn't difficult at all. Hector followed the procession of families walking down the street, their arms filled with flowers, candles, and food to bring to the graves.

Hector gasped as the cemetery came into view. What must have been hundreds of people filled the fenced-in lot. Each of the raised grave beds was covered with orange and red flowers made visible by flickering candles. It looked beautiful and eerie at the same time.

Hector wasn't sure how to find his family, so he wandered among the graves, searching the crowd, until he spotted Tia Rosa's mop of gray hair. He rushed to her.

"Hector!" she said. "I am glad you are feeling better. Abuela will be glad you are here."

Tia Rosa pointed to a nearby grave bed decorated with flowers and skulls. Abuela's photo sat on top of the flat stone at the head of the grave.

"Where is Eva?" Hector asked nervously.

Tia Rosa frowned. "She wandered off a little while ago. She was holding that silver skull you gave me. She seemed very interested in it."

"Which way did she go?" Hector asked.

Tia Rosa pointed to a dark corner of the cemetery, one bare of flowers and candles. "Over there, I think," she said.

"Thanks," Hector said, as he ran off to find Eva.

He felt another chill as he left the bright colors and lights and stepped into the dark corner. Thankfully, he spotted Eva right away. His sister was sitting at the foot of a large, stone crypt.

"Eva, what are you doing here?" Hector asked. Then he noticed his sister was holding the silver skull in her hands, staring at it.

"I'm not sure," Eva answered, not looking up at him.

"Let's get out of here and get back to Tia Rosa," Hector said. "It's creepy over here."

But Eva didn't move. "I can't explain it, but the skull likes it here," she said. Her voice sounded weak and a little strange. "It wants us to stay."

Hector's skin prickled. This didn't sound like his sister at all. The skull had some kind of hold on Eva.

"Snap out of it!" he said. "The skull might like it here, but I don't. Let's go get some tamales."

Eva looked up at her brother for the first time.

She looked terrified.

"Eva, what is it?" Hector asked.

Then Hector felt something cold and sharp grab his ankle. He looked down.

A skeleton hand had grabbed him by the ankle. Its long, bony arm extended into the crypt and then disappeared in the darkness.

"Eva!" Hector cried. He kicked his leg, but the skeletal hand did not let go. It yanked his leg with such force that Hector fell facedown in the dirt.

Scrambling, Hector reached out to grab his sister. But the skeleton yanked again, and Hector felt himself being pulled backward into the dark, dark crypt.

Eva watched her brother vanish and sat, stunned, for a moment. She looked down at the silver skull in her hands.

Light gleamed from its hollow eyes.

Eva felt a surge of energy. She jumped up. "Hector, I'm coming for you!" she called out. She placed the silver skull on the cold stone.

Then she hesitated. It seemed safer to leave the skull here, somehow. But what if the skull had something to do with all of this? She might need it if she was going to save Hector.

If Eva takes the skull into the crypt, go to page 73.

If Eva leaves the skull behind, go to page 111.

Continued from page 81

Hector didn't want to wait. He quickly threw the rosemary over his right shoulder.

"Wait!" Eva protested, but then she went ahead and did the same.

The ghost was floating closer. Eva and Hector both closed their eyes and turned in a circle to the left, three times in a row.

Hector made his final turn. "Did it work?" he asked, opening his eyes.

The hideous face of the ghost stared right at him.

"Aaaaaaaaaah!" Hector screamed.

And then he ran, ran as fast as he could, not caring where he was going. He could hear Eva's feet beside him. Hector ran past the ghost and down the street, which came to a dead end. There was an empty lot to the right. Hector scrambled over the fence and started to run across the lot.

And then, suddenly, the earth gave way beneath his feet. Hector felt himself falling, and then landed on soft ground with a thud. A second later, he heard Eva land next to him.

Hector wasn't hurt, just stunned. He stood up. They were in some kind of pit.

"Are you okay?" he asked Eva.

But his sister was staring right through him, a look of terror on her face. Hector turned around and let out a scream.

Two skeletons leaned against the far wall. One held a battered guitar in its hands. The other held two maracas.

"The twin brothers," Hector said. "We found them."

An evil laugh filled the pit. Hector looked up to see the evil ghost looking down at them, grinning with its wide mouth.

"I buried the bodies of these brothers years ago," said the ghost in a raspy voice. "And now you shall join them."

"No!" Hector cried. He tried to scramble up the side of the pit, but it was too steep.

There was a scraping sound as the evil ghost dragged a panel of wood over the opening of the pit. The starry sky was replaced by empty darkness.

"Don't panic," Eva said. "There's got to be a way out of here."

Hector took the *calaca* of the mariachi out of his pocket and held it in his hand. "Tia Rosa said this might help us," he said.

"We need a ladder," Eva said. "Or a telephone. Not a *calaca*."

"Someone will find us," Hector said hopefully. But he wasn't so sure.

Tia Rosa said no one had ever found the twin mariachi brothers.

"Help!" Hector screamed suddenly. "Help! Help! Help!"

But nobody heard him scream.

THE END

All the next day, Eva tried to convince her brother to go to the cemetery that night. But Hector didn't change his mind. He helped pile the finished tamales and empanadas onto plates and place them on the *ofrenda*. He listened while Tia Rosa told stories of Abuela as a little girl. But when it came time to carry the food and flowers and skulls to Abuela's grave, Hector pretended he was sick.

Eva frowned as Hector faked a stomachache, but she didn't tell her parents the truth, like she usually would have when her brother tried to get away with something. Hector seemed genuinely afraid of the skull. If he didn't want to go to the cemetery, that was his problem.

"I am glad you are not sick, too, Eva," Tia Rosa said. "Abuela will be glad to see one of her grandchildren from America. But I know Hector will be there in spirit."

Tia Rosa took the silver skull from the *ofrenda* and handed it to Eva. "Since you gave me such a beautiful skull, you can take the skulls to the cemetery," she said. "Find a plate and put the sugar skulls on there, too."

Eva was fascinated by the sugar skulls, which

were made of sugar, water, and meringue powder and packed into molds. They became rock hard when dry, and were decorated with colorful icing and foil. Some of the skulls had sequins stuck into the eye sockets. Tia Rosa had bought them at a shop in the city.

When everything was packed up, they said good-bye to Hector, who was dramatically clutching his stomach, and headed out into the street. Eva was surprised to see so many people out, their arms filled with baskets and platters of food and flowers. People greeted one another and chatted quietly as they walked to the cemetery.

As they approached, Eva saw that the cemetery was filled with light and people. The light came from candles placed on all of the graves, which were raised beds topped with thick blocks of stones at one end. In other parts of the cemetery, Eva saw stone crypts—they looked like little square houses, almost, but Eva knew there were coffins inside.

Tia Rosa led them to Abuela's grave—a neat, well-kept grave bed near the cemetery fence. Eva set up the skulls alongside the candles, food, and flowers that her parents and Tia Rosa set up. Finally, Tia Rosa placed the picture of Abuela in the center of it all.

"What happens next?" Eva asked.

"Now we will sit quietly for a while and remember Abuela," Tia Rosa said. "And then we will share the *ofrendas* with our neighbors here tonight."

Eva sat cross-legged on the grass and stared at Abuela's grave. She didn't have any memories of her grandmother, but she did remember the stories her mother and Tia Rosa had told her. She stared at the flickering candles and tried to conjure up one from her memory.

Oddly, she found her gaze drawn to the silver skull. As she stared into its hollow eyes, she had the sudden urge to pick it up. Without knowing exactly why, Eva took the skull off the grave.

Eva meant to sit back down in the grass, but she found herself wandering off, until she came to a nearby crypt. She sat at the crypt's edge, never taking her eyes off the skull.

"I feel like there's something you want to tell me," Eva whispered. "What is it?"

Suddenly, a greenish glow shone from the skull's eye sockets. Eva gasped. She looked all around. Could the skull be reflecting light from somewhere? But the crypt was secluded, far from the candlelight.

The green glow became stronger. Eva's hands trembled. Maybe Hector was right. There was something . . . supernatural about the skull.

The open mouth of the crypt beckoned to her. She could throw in the skull, turn around, and never look back. She and Hector would be rid of the skull forever.

If Eva throws the skull into the crypt, go to page 49.

If Eva decides to hold onto the skull, go to page 128.

Continued from page 26

"Hector, pick it up!" Eva said in that voice that Hector knew meant he'd better do what his sister said—or else. He reached down and picked up the skull.

"Are you happy?" he asked. He stuffed it in his duffel bag and zipped it shut. "We'll give it to Tia Rosa as soon as we land."

Immediately, the plane stopped shaking. Light streamed into the cabin. Hector looked out the window and saw a bright blue sky.

"Ladies and gentlemen, looks like we got through the storm just fine," the captain announced. "We should have a smooth ride the rest of the way."

Mrs. Ramirez stood up in her seat and turned to the twins. "Are you two all right?" she asked.

"We're fine," Eva called back.

Hector didn't feel fine. How had that skull ended up in his bag? Something weird was definitely going on. And he didn't like it one bit.

Hector was so worried about the skull that he forgot to worry about being on the plane. He didn't even notice when they landed. He and Eva waited patiently while the other passengers filed out of the plane. They reached their parents and headed out to the crowded terminal. A plump woman with a friendly smile and a curly mop of black hair streaked with gray pushed through the crowd toward them. She wore a bright pink dress.

"Tia Rosa!" Mrs. Ramirez cried. She and her aunt hugged each other. Tia Rosa gave Mr. Ramirez a hug, too. Then she turned to Hector and Eva.

"How big you are!" she said. "I haven't seen you since you were little babies."

She hugged them both tightly. Then she led them to the baggage claim area while they told her about the flight. When they got their luggage, Tia Rosa led them to her small yellow car in the parking lot. Hector and Eva squeezed in the back with their mother.

Hector got stuck in the middle—Eva always got the window when she wanted it—so he had to crane his neck to see the sights as they drove through downtown Mexico City.

"I thought we'd make a stop on the way," Tia Rosa said. "To get in the spirit of the Day of the Dead."

"Where are we going?" Eva asked.

"You'll see," Tia Rosa said, smiling in the rearview mirror.

A few minutes later, Tia Rosa parked the car on a busy street full of shops.

Hector gasped to see skeleton faces staring back at him from every window. The window of a bakery was painted with laughing and playing skeletons. Another shop window held rows of grinning skull masks. They piled out of the car, and Tia Rosa led them to a shop filled with small cases of small white skulls. The skulls were painted with colorful designs, like circles and flowers. Some had sequins in the eye sockets. Others had strips of colorful foil attached. And still others, Hector saw, had names written across their foreheads.

"Sugar skulls!" Eva said happily.

Of course, Hector realized. He had seen pictures of them, but never so many at once.

While Eva and Hector looked at the skulls in the glass case, Tia Rosa walked up to the counter. She came back holding a small parcel. She reached inside and handed Eva and Hector a skull.

Hector looked at his. His own name, "Hector," was written in green icing across the skull's forehead. He looked at Eva, and saw hers bore her name, too.

"When we eat a skull with our name on it, we take in our own mortality," Tia Rosa explained. "In Mexico, we know that life and death are like brother and sister. Two members of the same family. Like you and Eva."

"Aren't they too sweet to eat?" Mrs. Ramirez asked.

"Very sweet," said Tia Rosa. "But something tells me Hector will not have a problem."

Hector grinned. "Nothing is too sweet for me!"

"You can say that again," Eva added.

As they walked to the car, Eva whispered in Hector's ear. "We should give Tia Rosa the silver skull now. To thank her for the sugar skulls."

Hector hesitated. As much as he wanted to get rid of the silver skull, he was really starting to like Tia Rosa a lot. If there was something wrong with the skull, he didn't want to pass it on to his aunt.

"Fine," Eva said. "Then I'll give it to her."

When they got to the car, Eva opened Hector's duffel bag and took out the silver skull. She handed it to Tia Rosa in the front seat.

"Thank you for the sugar skulls," she said. "This is a present from me and Hector. For the *ofrenda*."

For a second, a clouded look passed over Tia Rosa's face. Then she smiled—but Hector didn't think she looked very happy.

"I am glad to see you are in the spirit of Day of the Dead," Tia Rosa said. "This will go perfectly on Abuela's altar."

Tia Rosa put the skull in her handbag. Then she navigated the car through the downtown area, which seemed to be packed with more cars than Hector had ever seen. When they left the heart of the city, the traffic opened up a bit, and Tia Rosa was able to go a little faster.

Then, suddenly, there was a loud popping sound, and the car lurched. Tia Rosa slowed down and pulled to the side of the road.

"Sounds like a flat tire," said Mr. Ramirez. "Let me help."

He and Tia Rosa got out of the car and fixed the tire. While he waited, Hector couldn't help thinking about the skull.

First the pizza accident. Then the turbulence on the plane. And now a flat tire. Was the skull to blame somehow? It was worrying him more and more.

It didn't take long to change the tire, and they soon made their way to Tia Rosa's neighborhood in Coyoacán. Tia Rosa stopped in front of a small house painted bright blue.

Inside, the first thing Hector noticed was the large *ofrenda* in the living room. The *ofrenda* was a table covered with a white cloth and then topped by two boxes covered in white, each smaller than the other, so that the shape of the *ofrenda* was like a wedding cake. A framed picture of a woman with gray hair sat in the center on the very top layer. The picture was flanked by two purple candles and two vases filled with orange flowers. The other layers were so filled that Hector could barely take in all that was there. He saw skulls, skeleton figures, apples, oranges, more orange flowers, and a glass of water.

Tia Rosa saw Hector staring at it and smiled. "Yes, it's very beautiful," she said. "I will tell you about it in a little while. But first, we will eat. You all must be very hungry."

Tia Rosa fed them chicken and tortillas and rice and had bottles of sweet, syrupy soda pop for Hector and Eva, which Hector thought was delicious. When they were done, Tia Rosa showed them the *ofrenda*.

She explained that the orange flowers were *cempasúchil*—marigolds. Their strong scent was supposed to lure the spirits of the ancestors back home. The glass of water was to quench the spirits' thirst. The apples and oranges were to feed the spirits of the ancestors, who would be hungry from their long journey back to the living world.

"And tonight you will help me make tamales for the *ofrenda*, as well," she said. "They were your Abuela's favorite."

Tia Rosa started to lead them away, but Eva stopped her.

"Don't forget about the silver skull we gave you," Eva said.

"Oh, yes," Tia Rosa said. Hector could tell she was trying to smile again. "Of course."

She fetched the silver skull from her handbag and placed it on the altar.

"There," she said. "It will be just fine there." Hector thought her voice sounded unsure.

But she was smiling again soon enough, when they were all crowded in the kitchen to make the tamales. Tia Rosa showed them the dried corn husks, which had been soaking in water to soften them up. On the stove was a bubbling pot of seasoned meat filling.

"I will show you how to fold the tamales like experts," she said. Then she went to the stove to get the pot of filling.

The next few seconds seemed to happen in slow motion. Hector's father moved his arm, knocking over a glass of water on the table. Tia Rosa turned around from the stove and stepped in the water. There was a horrible crash as she slid to the floor.

"Tia Rosa!" Mrs. Ramirez screamed.

Hector's parents helped her up. "I am fine," she said. Then she looked at the floor and her face fell.

The pot of the tamale filling had turned over completely, spilling everywhere.

"I suppose we can make the tamales tomorrow,

if we wake up early," she said.

"Of course, Tia," Hector's mother said. "We'll help you."

Hector pulled Eva aside.

"This can't be a coincidence," he whispered. "Something is up with that skull. I think we should tell Tia Rosa about what happened yesterday."

"Don't be silly, Hector," Eva said. "I keep telling you—that skull isn't making bad things happen. It's not possible!"

If Hector tells Tia Rosa about the silver skull, go to page 51.

If Hector doesn't tell Tia Rosa about the silver skull, go to page 82.

Continued from page 57

Eva wasn't sure what to do, so she grabbed the skull.

Better safe than sorry, Eva thought.

Then she ducked and ran into the crypt. The skull's eyes were still gleaming, so Eva could at least see where she was going. Wispy cobwebs covered the stone walls on either side of her. She looked down at the path in front of her, and saw that it sloped sharply downward.

The skeleton had taken Hector down there somewhere, under the ground, Eva realized. She took a deep breath and began the climb down. A stale, earthy smell filled her nostrils as she climbed deeper and deeper.

And then, suddenly, the path opened up into a round chamber. Her brother sat on the dirt floor, looking dazed.

He was surrounded by skeletons.

Living skeletons.

Eva knew right away that these weren't the plastic skeletons you see in a Halloween shop. They were bent over Hector, clicking the fingers of their bony hands together, as if in anticipation of something. Their yellowing bones were streaked with dirt, moss, and cobwebs.

And then, all at once, they turned and looked at Eva. Or that's what she thought, for she soon saw that they were all staring at the silver skull.

One of the skeletons took a step forward, and Eva heard its bones creak with the effort. Then its lower jaw began to move up and down, and Eva realized she heard a voice talking in her head. The voice sounded low and raspy, like wind rattling through the bare branches of trees in late autumn.

"It hasss come to ussss at lassst," the skeleton said.

For a split second, Eva felt her head grow cloudy, and she thought she might melt to the floor in a heap. But she pulled herself together.

"You mean the skull?" Eva asked. The sound of her own voice surprised her. "What do you want with it?"

"We want to ressstore the balansss," the skeleton replied.

Restore the balance? She didn't know what that meant, but it didn't sound bad. "Fine," Eva said, holding out the skull. "Give me back my brother, and I'll give you the skull."

"Eva, no!" Hector cried. "They're going to do something bad with it. I can feel it!"

Eva pulled back her hand.

"All right," she said. "Tell me the whole story.

Or no skull."

"It issss ssssimple," said the skeleton, and as it spoke, Eva saw a worm crawl out of its eye socket. "We are the ssspiritssss of thossse who are not fed. Thossse who are not honored. For yearsss our ssspiritssss have languissshed with no one to honor usss. And now we will take what isss ourssss."

Eva remembered something that Tia Rosa had told them at the *ofrenda*. That it was the duty of those living to honor the ancestors on the Day of the Dead. In one of the books she had read, Eva remembered a folktale about spirits who had become angry when no *ofrendas* were made for them. Just like these spirits.

"What do you mean, take what is yours?" Eva asked.

"Life," the skeleton said simply. "We have been denied for ssso long. But with the sssilver sssskull, we can gain life forssss again. Firssst from the boy. And then, from you."

It didn't take Eva long to figure out what would happen to her and Hector if the skeletons took their life force. She ran to Hector's side.

"Come on," she said, helping her brother up. "We've got to get out of here."

The skeletons drew closer, reaching out with their long, bony fingers, but Eva didn't flinch.

They were just a bunch of rickety bones, she told herself. She and Hector could easily push through them.

Hector leaned against her, and Eva could see that his ankle had twisted when the skeletons dragged him into the crypt.

"Put your arm around me," Eva whispered. "We're going to push our way out of here."

Eva scanned the chamber. The path she had taken down might be too steep for Hector to climb with his hurt ankle. But just to her left was another path that looked straight. She didn't know where it led—but as long as it took them away from the skeletons, she'd be happy.

Eva and Hector had taken their first step forward when the skull's eyes began to glow more intensely than before. The skull whirled around in Eva's hand, zapping Hector and Eva with the light beams. Eva felt as though her whole body was frozen. Instinctively, she closed her eyes, and she found she was able to move.

"Hector, don't look at it!" she cried.

"Can't you just drop it?" Hector asked.

"If I do, they'll only use it to steal someone else's life force," she said. "Let's go."

But the skeletons were on top of them now. Sharp fingers tore at their clothing. Eva pushed forward.

She knew she had to make a decision fast. The sloped path was closer, but the straight path might be easier for Hector. Which way should they go?

If the twins escape using the sloped path, go to page 86.
If the twins escape using the straight path, go to page 101.

Continued from page 140

"Maybe we should wake Tia Rosa," Hector said. "That was a good idea."

Eva nodded. "All right. Maybe the music is coming from somewhere in her neighborhood. She'll probably know just what to do."

The twins tiptoed upstairs and quietly knocked on Tia Rosa's bedroom door. Their aunt opened the door for them a few seconds later, wearing a pink robe. Her curly hair looked disheveled.

"Is everything all right?" she asked.

"We can hear music downstairs," Hector said. "It's coming from outside. We heard it last night, too. And in Bleaktown."

"In Bleaktown?" Tia Rosa asked. "But how can it be the same music?"

Hector shook his head. "I'm not sure."

"The music is playing now," Eva said. "Come hear it."

Tia Rosa followed them downstairs. Hector could hear the fast melody of the guitars, the high notes of the trumpet, and the fast percussion beat.

"Can you hear it?" Hector asked.

Tia Rosa shook her head. "No," she said thoughtfully. "But I think there is a reason you might be able to. Come, sit down. Tell me all that has happened."

Hector thought it was strange that Tia Rosa couldn't hear the music, but he was relieved that she didn't think they were making it up, either. They all sat down in the living room and Hector and Eva told the story of following the music the night before and running away from the creepy-looking ghost.

Tia Rosa nodded. "Just as I thought," she said. She got up, walked over to the *ofrenda*, and returned with the *calaca* of the mariachis. "I have a story to tell you.

"Years ago, twin brothers came to Mexico City from the countryside," she began. "They were mariachis. One played guitar, and the other played percussion. People traveled from all over just to hear them play their music. No one could play like those brothers.

"But some were jealous of their talent. That is always the way. And one night, on the Day of the Dead, the brothers disappeared. People suspected that something evil had befallen them. They were never seen again."

"That's so sad!" Eva said.

Tia Rosa nodded. "Yes, it is," she said. "But there is more. It is said that when the Day of the Dead draws near, the brothers play their music, hoping that someone will discover where they are.

But because the brothers were twins, only twins are able to hear it."

Hector and Eva looked at each other. Twins. Just like them.

Tia Rosa held out the *calaca*. "I think there is a reason you bought this *calaca*," she said. "It is a sign. A sign that you must help the lost mariachi brothers."

She handed the *calaca* to Hector. "Follow the music," she said. "And take this with you. It may help you."

Hector gulped. "Follow the music? Tonight? But what if we see that creepy ghost again?"

Tia Rosa frowned. "That part troubles me. The mariachis were good men. The ghost must be connected to them somehow. One moment."

Tia Rosa got up and hurried to the kitchen. She came back holding a fistful of what looked like spiky green leaves.

"Take this rosemary," she said. "Each of you. When the ghost is near, throw a stalk over your left shoulder. Then close your eyes, turn to the right, and circle around three times. This will cause the ghost to disappear. Something my own abuela taught me years ago."

Hector and Eva each took a handful of the rosemary stalks. Eva took a deep breath.

"I guess we should go," she said. "I want to

help those poor brothers."

Hector and Eva slipped on their sneakers. Tia Rosa hugged them both tightly.

"Be careful," she said. "I would not send you out if I did not believe you were meant to do this. The *calaca* is a sign."

Hector and Eva stepped out into the night. Stars shone brightly in the sky above. Once again, they followed the music down the streets of Tia Rosa's neighborhood.

Just like the night before, they followed the music down a side street. And just like the night before, they saw the ghostly figure of the man floating toward them.

Hector held up his rosemary. "Okay," he said. "When he gets near, we throw the rosemary over our right shoulder, right? Then we circle three times to the left."

Eva frowned. "I think it's the opposite," she said. "Throw the rosemary on the left, and circle on the right."

"We'd better decide fast," Hector said. "The ghost is getting closer!"

If the twins do what Eva remembered, go to page 37.

If the twins do what Hector remembered, go to page 58.

Continued from page 72

"It's a nice present," Eva continued. "Don't spoil it by telling Tia Rosa some crazy story."

Hector sighed. Why did he always let Eva win every argument?

"All right," he said. "But if one more bad thing happens—"

"Nothing bad will happen," his sister promised.

The twins helped clean up the mess on the floor. Instead of making the tamales, they all sat in the living room. Tia Rosa told stories about her sister, Hector and Eva's grandmother, and what she was like as a little girl.

"Marcela was always the brave one," Tia Rosa said. "Never afraid of anything. Me, I was frightened by even the littlest noise."

Mr. Ramirez looked at Eva and Hector. "Sounds like two children I know."

Hector's face flushed. It was bad enough that lots of things scared him. It was worse when people found out about it.

"Don't worry, Hector," Tia Rosa said. "You will grow out of it. I did."

Hector tried to change the subject. "So will the spirits of the ancestors really come back tomorrow?" he asked.

"That is what many have believed, since ancient times," she said. "Some say the ancestors come to us in spirit form. Others say they take the form of animals. That is why it is bad luck to harm any animals on the Day of the Dead."

"Cool," Hector said. The more he learned about the holiday, the less creepy it seemed to him. He had to admit it was all pretty interesting—maybe even more interesting than stuffing himself with candy on Halloween.

Suddenly, there was a loud crash from the entryway. Hector turned just in time to see a green glow coming from the eyes of the silver skull. At the same time, the top layer of the tiered *ofrenda* came crashing down. Apples and oranges bounced off the tables and landed on the floor.

"Oh, my!" Tia Rosa exclaimed. She ran to the *ofrenda* just as the light from the silver skull's eyes began to die out.

Hector waited for someone to say something about the skull, but no one did. They might not have seen it. Everyone busily began to pick up the fallen fruit from the altar.

"So many accidents tonight," Tia Rosa said, eyeing the skull as she spoke.

"Yes," Hector said, shooting a look at his sister. "*Too* many accidents."

Eva rolled her eyes. "Can I talk to you outside,

please?"

Mrs. Ramirez shook her head. "More twin stuff, eh? Go on, you two."

Eva and Hector stepped out into the night. The very last of the sun's rays gave the sky a warm glow.

"Hector, it was just an accident," she said. "Accidents happen."

"But I saw the skull's eyes glow again!" Hector protested. "Just like last night!"

"Well, I didn't see anything," Eva said.

"I'm telling you, Eva," Hector insisted. "That skull makes bad things happen! We have to stop it!"

"He's right!"

Both twins jumped a little at the sound of a strange voice. It sounded like a squawk.

Hector looked around.

"Who's there?" he asked.

He suddenly felt a rush of air next to his face, and to his surprise, a parrot perched on his shoulder.

"It's your abuela, Marcela," squawked the parrot.

"I know parrots can talk, but that's pretty amazing," Eva said.

The parrot flew to Eva and fluttered around her face. "Didn't you listen to anything my sister told you?" she asked. "Spirits can take the form of animals. That includes parrots."

Eva opened her mouth to reply, then shut it. For once, Hector thought, his sister had nothing to say.

The parrot settled back on Hector's shoulder. "You are right about the skull, *hijo*. It is bad. Very bad. And the accidents it is causing are making the spirits of the ancestors angry. It is ruining their feast!"

"I knew it," Hector said smugly.

"You must get rid of the skull tonight," she said. "In the cemetery. It is the only way."

Hector didn't like the sound of that. "The cemetery? Tonight?"

In the meantime, Eva had begun whispering to herself. "It's only my imagination. It's only my imagination," she said over and over.

If Hector and Eva take the silver skull to the cemetery, go to page 104.

If Hector and Eva ignore the talking parrot, go to page 115.

Continued from page 77

A bony finger scratched Eva's face, and she made a split-second decision. Pulling Hector and holding the skull with one hand, she ran for the nearest exit—the sloped path.

But the path was too narrow for both of them to climb side by side, so Eva pushed Hector in front of her. He limped up the hill, but even with Eva pushing, it wasn't fast enough. Eva felt two skeleton hands grab her ankles.

"Let go of me!" Eva screamed, but their grip was tight, and she felt herself slipping. Without thinking, she let go of the silver skull to get a grip on the dirt path. The skull tumbled over her, right back down the path.

Then suddenly, she saw Hector seem to fly up the path. The next thing she knew, she felt two strong arms grab hers.

Eva looked up to see her father's face. "I've got you, honey," he said, and as he pulled her up, the skeletons released her ankles.

They got what they wanted, Eva thought. *But there's nothing I can do about that now.*

Seconds later, she found herself outside again, back in the fresh air. Tia Rosa had wrapped a blanket around Hector, and her mother was looking at Hector's ankle.

Tia Rosa was shaking her head. "I saw you run into the crypt, Eva," she said. "What were you thinking?"

Hector and Eva looked at each other. Would the adults believe their story?

Then Hector spoke up. "I tripped and fell into the crypt," he said. "Eva was just trying to save me."

"That's right," Eva said quickly. "But then I got stuck down there, too."

Tia Rosa gave them a look that said she didn't quite believe them. But that look changed to relief.

"I am glad you are all right," she said. "Let us get you home. I will see if the doctor can come look at Hector's ankle."

"It feels better," Hector said, standing up. "See? I can walk on it."

They headed home after gathering up some of the items from Abuela's grave. Tia Rosa passed out the food to others in the cemetery as they left.

Eva and Hector hung slightly behind as the adults walked up ahead.

"Thanks for coming to save me," Hector told his sister.

"I almost made things worse," Eva replied. "I should never have taken that skull with me."

"What happened to the skull, anyway?" Hector asked.

Eva bit her lip. "I dropped it," she said nervously. "In the chamber. But I am sure everything's fine."

"Right," Hector said, but his voice sounded unsure. "Everything's fine."

Then, suddenly, a familiar voice hissed inside Eva's head.

"Thisss isss not over."

Eva stopped. Her whole body shook with cold.

"Where are you?" she whispered. But she knew the answer.

The skeleton laughed a sharp, hissing laugh. "With you, Eva," the skeleton said. "With you!"

THE END

Continued from page 44

Hector didn't even look back at the altar. He went right into the living room, changed into his pajamas, and covered himself with blankets.

Despite what had happened, Hector fell into a deep sleep right away. The next time he woke up, sun was streaming in through the windows.

I'm glad that night's over, Hector thought, sitting up. He turned to where his sister's blankets were set up. Now that the sun was shining, he wanted to find out what had happened at the cemetery last night.

But Eva's blankets were neatly folded on the couch, just as they had been the day before.

"Eva?" Hector asked. He scrambled to his feet. She must have slept upstairs last night, Hector guessed. He had no idea how early it was; maybe everyone was upstairs sleeping.

Hector passed the *ofrenda* on his way to the stairs and noticed that the marigold flowers had dissolved into petals, which had scattered all over the white tablecloth. No message there.

He headed upstairs. To his surprise, he found that all of the bedrooms were empty and the beds were made.

Almost like nobody had come home last night,

Hector realized. He felt a strange sense of foreboding.

Hector ran down the stairs and stopped in front of the *ofrenda*. Somehow, he knew the answer to what had happened was there.

There were the scattered flower petals. And the *calacas*: the man and woman, the mermaid, and the doctor.

And four others.

Four more? Hector hadn't remembered seeing any more *calacas*. He bent down to get a closer look.

One skeleton figure was plump, dressed in pink, and topped with gray curly hair. The others were a man and a woman with dark hair. And the fourth one was smaller, a girl about Hector's age, with dark hair. Hector leaned closer. The girl skeleton was wearing jeans and a purple shirt. Just like Eva had worn yesterday.

Hector felt like he couldn't breathe. The plump woman, the couple, the girl—they looked just like his family. With a cry, Hector ran to the front door. It couldn't be. His family was out there, somewhere.

He almost bumped into a kindly looking woman walking up the stairs.

"Tia Rosa!" Hector cried frantically. "Have you seen her?"

The woman frowned. "That is why I am here," she said. "Your tia went missing at the cemetery last night. So did her family from America. We have been looking for them all night. I hoped they had come back here."

Hector slowly turned his head and looked at the *calacas* on the altar. They grinned back at him.

"Oh, they're here, all right," Hector said, sinking down onto the steps.

Someone, or something, had tried to warn him.

But he hadn't listened.

THE END

Continued from page 36

As soon as they arrived back home, Hector wanted to take the skull back to Sebastian Cream's Junk Shop. He and Eva hurried downtown, past trick-or-treaters dressed as ghosts and superheroes. But when they got there, the sign on the junk shop read CLOSED.

"Maybe we could just leave the skull here," Hector said.

"Someone might take it," Eva warned.

"Good," Hector said. "I don't even care if I get my money back. If someone else wants it, they can have it."

So Hector left the skull in front of the Scream Shop door. Then he turned around and didn't look back. It was still early. He could get some trick-or-treating in after all.

Eva didn't want to go, so Hector threw on an old coat of his dad's and some monster makeup and went on his own. When he came back, he held a pillowcase bursting with candy. Hector ate a bunch of it before falling asleep. Thankfully, he didn't dream of the skull.

The next morning, Hector rummaged through his candy bag for an after-breakfast snack. His hand landed on something smooth and cold.

Hector snatched his hand away. It couldn't be. It just couldn't. He opened the bag wide and looked in.

The silver skull looked up at him, surrounded by pieces of candy.

"No!" Hector cried. Without waiting, he grabbed the bag and ran out the door. He ran straight to Wary Lane and through the open door of Sebastian Cream's Junk Shop. Then he slammed the pillow-case on the counter.

Mr. Cream looked up at him through his glasses.

"Returning the skull?" he asked.

"Yes!" Hector cried, exasperated. "I don't want my money back. I just don't want the skull back. I never want to see it again."

"Ah," said Mr. Cream, reaching into the drawer of his register. "But you purchased the skull. Unless I give you back your money, it will always be yours."

Mr. Cream handed Hector fifteen dollars. Then he picked up the bag.

"What about your candy?" he asked.

"Keep it," Hector said, backing up. "Just keep it."

Hector stepped outside and looked behind him. "I will never go in that place again," he said.

Then he ran home as fast as he could.

THE END

Continued from page 22

Eva grabbed Hector by the shoulder. "Listen to yourself!" she snapped. "You don't have to follow that music anywhere. Do you want to ruin this whole trip?"

Hector realized Eva was right. What was he thinking, leaving Tia Rosa's house in the middle of the night?

"Sorry," he said.

Then he and Eva both climbed back into bed.

The music did not stop. In fact, Hector thought, it was getting louder.

He gripped the covers, resisting the urge to get up and follow it.

Instead, he followed the sound as it seemed to get closer and closer to the house.

Eva had not fallen asleep yet, either. "It must be some noisy neighbors or something," she said. "Maybe Tia Rosa will hear it and do something about it."

Then, suddenly, the music stopped.

"See," Eva said. "Nothing to worry about."

And then Tia Rosa's front door opened.

Two skeletons walked through the door.

They were dressed just like the mariachis in

the *calaca*. One carried a trumpet, and the other carried a guitar.

Hector was too shocked to cry out.

The skeletons did not even look at Hector and Eva.

They headed straight for the *ofrenda*. In the candlelight, Hector could see that one of the skeletons was reaching toward the *calaca* with a long, bony finger.

The finger touched the *calaca*, and there was a strange, sizzling sound. The next instant, two more skeletons stood in Tia Rosa's living room. Another guitar player, and a mariachi playing maracas.

Just like the calaca *we bought*, Hector thought. *It's come to life!*

The four skeletons turned toward Hector and Eva. They nodded in unison. Then one by one, they filed back outside. The last skeleton shut the door behind them. Seconds later, the twins heard the mariachi music start up again. It slowly faded away.

Hector and Eva looked at each other, stunned. The hall light came on, and Tia Rosa came down the stairs, yawning.

"Are you all right?" she asked. "I thought I heard a noise."

"We're fine, Tia Rosa," Eva said.

"Right," Hector said. "I just had a weird dream, that's all."

After all, would she have believed the real story?

THE END

"You do what you want," Hector told Eva. "I'm running toward that music!"

"Hector, wait!" Eva yelled. But she followed him, anyway.

They turned and ran back down the narrow street. It looked like a dead end. Hector grew nervous. Had he made the right choice?

And then the ghostly figure appeared in front of them again. Its gaping mouth formed into a snarl. Hector's first instinct was to turn and run again. But the pull of the music was too strong.

Hector grabbed Eva's arm. "Don't stop!" he yelled.

Eva was too shocked to protest. Hector led his sister, full speed, right toward the ghostly figure. Holding his breath, he ran past the figure as fast as he could. The right side of his body, closest to the specter, felt icy cold for a brief second.

And then they were at the end of the street. Hector could see that although it was a dead end, there was an empty lot, overgrown with weeds, to the right. The music was coming from there. Hector and Eva scrambled over the low, broken fence that surrounded the lot.

"Help!" Hector cried. "Is somebody there?"

And then the earth gave way beneath Hector's feet. Hector felt himself falling into some kind of hole. He landed with a thud, in the dirt. A second later, Eva thudded next to him.

"Are you okay?" he asked his sister.

Eva nodded, brushing dirt off her jeans. "I think—aaaaaaaaaah!"

Hector followed Eva's gaze. They weren't in a hole at all.

They were in some kind of grave. Two piles of bones were stacked up inches away from them. Each stack was topped with a grinning skull.

Hector's first thought was that they should get out—fast. But before he could move, the bones began to float into the air. Hector and Eva watched, transfixed, as each pile of bones formed into a perfect skeleton.

"We knew you would come," said the skeletons in one voice. Hector wasn't sure where it was coming from, exactly. Did skeletons have voice boxes?

"Who-who are you?" Hector asked, his voice shaking.

"We are the lost brothers," said the skeletons. "Once, we were alive. So alive! We played our music for men, women, and children. We made people laugh and dance."

"Mariachis," Eva whispered softly.

"The best mariachis in Mexico," the skeletons said. "But our lives were cut short by a man jealous of our talents. He stole our lives. Then he buried us here, where no one could find us. And now he watches over us, to make sure no one ever will."

Hector thought of the ghostly figure that had tried to stop them. "You mean that ghost?"

The skeleton brothers nodded in unison. "We have waited, here in this lonely grave, for someone who could hear the music of our spirits. Twins, just like us."

"We're twins," Eva said.

"And only you can help us now," said the brothers. "The man buried our instruments away from us, so that we would never again make beautiful music. You heard the music of our souls. But we need to play our real instruments again. Only when we do that will we rest in peace."

"How can we help?" Hector asked.

"Our instruments are buried somewhere in this lot," they said. "Find them and bring them to us. That is all we need."

Hector and Eva looked at each other.

"It doesn't sound too hard," Hector said. He hoisted himself over the top of the grave to get a good look at the lot. It wasn't very big at all.

And then he saw the ghostly figure floating

toward him, a look of anger on his horrible face. Hector jumped back into the grave.

"It's back," he told Eva. "Maybe we should get out of here!"

If the twins leave, go to page 40.

If the twins agree to help the brothers, go to page 109.

Continued from page 77

Eva didn't think Hector could make it up the slope. She turned and ran with Hector toward the other path. She just hoped it didn't lead to a dead end.

They could hear the sound of the skeletons' bones clattering behind them as they ran. The light from the skull's eyes began to glow again. Hector quickly grabbed it from his sister and stuffed it into his front pocket.

"Good thinking," Eva said.

The path ahead curved sharply to the right. Eva guided Hector around the turn.

And then the path suddenly ended. The twins stopped just short of running right into a wall of musty earth. Panicked, Eva quickly turned around.

The living skeletons had turned the corner. The lead skeleton, who stood in front of the pack, held out its arms, stopping them. Its voice hissed in Eva's head.

"There isss no essscape," it promised.

Eva took a deep breath. There was only one way out—through the skeletons. They weren't going to get her—or the silver skull—without a fight.

But then she heard Hector shout next to her.

"Ancestors! Help us!" he cried. "Please help us!"

Eva didn't know what her brother was doing. "Hector, what—" she started.

And then the dark chamber filled with a light so bright that Eva had to shade her eyes. The skeletons let out a strange wail.

Then shadowy figures became visible in the light. They were men and women, old and young. One woman with curly hair looked a lot like Tia Rosa.

The army of shadow figures swirled around the skeletons. Then the bright light flashed even brighter, and Eva had to close her eyes.

When she opened them, she saw a pile of ashes in place where the skeletons had been. The chamber was dark again, and quiet.

She turned to her brother. "Hector, are you okay?"

Hector nodded. "Fine," he said. "Come on. Let's get out of here."

They walked back to the sloped path, feeling their way in the dark. Eva helped Hector up the hill and back out into the fresh air. Then they both collapsed against the cold wall of the crypt.

"How did you know to call the ancestors?" Eva asked, when she finally caught her breath.

"Something Tia Rosa said last night," Hector

said. "She said the ancestors come back on the Day of the Dead to protect us."

Eva was impressed. Why hadn't she remembered that? Then she thought of something.

"Hey," she said. "Do you still have the skull?"

Hector tapped his pocket. "Yup," he said. "Hey, maybe we can throw it away now. The skeletons are gone."

"Well, we can't give it back to Tia Rosa," Eva said. "I'll tell her we lost it. But I don't think we should throw it away."

"Why not?" Hector asked.

"It's too dangerous," Eva replied. "You never know. Maybe other skeletons would try to use it, too. I think we should take it back to that weird shop and ask the owner what he knows about it."

Hector frowned. "All right," he said. "But let's go as soon as we get home. I want to get rid of it as soon as we can!"

Go to page 143.

Hector was nervous about going to the cemetery. But Abuela's warning sounded serious. He didn't want to ignore it.

Even if he had to do it alone.

"I will take the skull to the cemetery tonight, Abuela," Hector said bravely.

Eva stopped muttering to herself. "What are you saying, Hector? Are you going to listen to a talking parrot?" she snapped.

"I'm going to listen to our abuela," Hector said. "This is not our imagination. And you know it."

Eva frowned. "I'm not sure. But if you're going to go ahead with this crazy plan, then I'd better go with you. You'll probably need my help."

Hector smiled. Eva would never admit he was right. But this was pretty close.

"What do we need to do?" Hector asked the parrot.

"You must go to the cemetery before midnight," Abuela said. "Look for a crypt with the name Vida engraved into it. Place the skull on the crypt. Walk around the crypt three times clockwise and say the words '*malo no mas*' seven times. When you are done, the skull will lose its power."

"Should we write this down or something?" Hector asked.

"I'll remember it," Eva said quickly.

"And I will be with you," Abuela said. "Go back inside now. But come to me as soon as you can. And bring the skull!"

When Hector and Eva got back inside, the *ofrenda* had been put back together. It was late, so Tia Rosa gave them blankets and pillows so they could sleep in the living room. Mr. and Mrs. Ramirez were sleeping in the guest room upstairs, next to Tia Rosa's room.

"Perfect," Hector whispered to his sister. "It will be easy to leave and meet Abuela."

It seemed like hours before the adults went upstairs to sleep, leaving Hector and Eva in the flickering candlelight of the *ofrenda*. When everything was quiet, they carefully slipped on jeans and shirts. Hector took the silver skull off of the *ofrenda*. They quietly opened the door and stepped outside.

It was dark out, so Hector didn't see Abuela approach, but he felt the parrot fly by his face and land on his shoulder.

"Turn right down the street," Abuela said. "I will lead you there."

They walked in silence down the streets of Coyoacán. Soon the cemetery came into view. Hector could make out the shapes of stones atop raised grave beds. In other parts of the cemetery were slabs of stones put together to make what looked like large boxes.

"Those are the crypts," Abuela said. "Find the one that says *Vida*."

They stepped onto the cemetery grounds, and Hector felt a shiver go up his spine. Cemeteries were creepy enough in the daytime. But now he could imagine a ghost behind every gravestone. As he walked toward the crypts, he imagined all the skeletons buried deep beneath the earth, right underneath his feet.

"I think we should split up to find the crypt," Eva suggested.

"No," Hector said quickly. "Let's stick together."

It was difficult to do in the dark, but soon their eyes adjusted. It wasn't long before they found the crypt marked "Vida."

"Put down the skull," Abuela instructed.

There was a low slab of stone in front of the crypt. Hector rested the skull there.

Immediately, green light flashed from its eyes. The ground beneath their feet began to shake. Hector could see gravestones trembling all around him.

"The skull is resisting," Abuela said. "We must act fast."

A cold, white mist began to rise up from the ground. It had a sour, musty smell.

"We have to walk around the crypt three times, right?" Eva asked.

"That's right," Abuela said. "Clockwise."

The ground began to shake again, harder this time. Hector could feel Abuela flap her wings on his shoulder.

"I can't hold on, *hijos*!" Abuela cried. "My spirit cannot stay in this body any longer. It is the skull. It is—"

And then the parrot squawked loudly, flapped its wings, and flew away.

"Abuela!" Hector cried.

"Quick," Eva said. "We'd better do this fast."

The twins began to walk around the crypt. As the mist grew thicker and thicker, it grew harder and harder to see. But they made it around three times and ended up back in front of the skull.

"Now we have to say something seven times, right?" Hector asked.

Eva bit her lip. "Right," she said. "*Mas malo mas*. No, that's not it. Maybe it's *malo no mas*."

"I thought you said you would remember!" Hector cried.

"I did, I think," she said. "Let's just pick one and try it."

If the twins say "*malo no mas*" seven times, go to page 131.

If the twins say "*mas malo mas*" seven times, go to page 125.

"He will not harm you," said the skeletons. "He has no power except to keep us in our lonely grave forever. But you can help us break that."

Hector nodded. "Okay," he said. He hoped the skeletons were telling the truth. But their story had moved him. If he could help them, he would.

Hector and Eva climbed out of the grave. They found a rusty old shovel leaning against the fence. The evil ghost floated around them, wailing in low, angry tones.

"Where should we start?" Hector asked.

"I've been thinking," Eva said. "The brothers said we were able to hear their music because they're twins. Maybe that will help us find the instruments, too."

Hector was puzzled. "What do you mean?"

"I'm not sure, exactly," Eva said. She grabbed her brother's hand. "Let's try."

Eva slowly led Hector around the lot. They walked around the perimeter, then made a smaller path inside the first path. They were going around a third time when suddenly Hector felt his whole body tingle. He looked at Eva.

"I felt it, too," Eva said.

"Don't move," said Hector. "I'll get the shovel."

Hector got the shovel and ran back to the spot. They took turns digging until they unearthed what they were looking for: an old, dirt-covered guitar and two maracas. Hector and Eva each grabbed an instrument and ran back to the grave.

The skeletons smiled up at them. "Thank you," they said, taking the instruments. Then they began to play.

The music was the same as before, but louder, and more real, somehow. As the mariachis played, their skeleton bones began to glow with golden light. Hector watched, amazed, as their bodies slowly floated up and out of the graves.

The evil ghost let out a scream, and in the next instant, vanished.

And the brothers kept playing. They floated up and up until they were higher than the tree-tops.

"Thank you," they called down. "We are at peace now."

Hector and Eva watched as the brothers disappeared into the night sky.

"You're welcome," Hector whispered.

THE END

Eva decided to play it safe. She left the skull where it was and then ran inside the crypt. It was impossible to see more than a few inches in front of her in the dark, so she reached out and touched the walls on either side of her. They felt cold and slimy, but she resisted the urge to pull her hands away. It was the only way to find Hector.

Eva followed a path straight for a few feet, and then changed direction as the path turned sharply. She noticed that the path had suddenly become steeper. She was going down, deep underground. And somewhere down there was Hector.

Soon Eva saw a faint glow in the distance. She slowed her pace and made a point to move quietly. She didn't want whatever got Hector to get her, too.

The path ended, and Eva saw that it opened up into a small chamber. She stifled a gasp as she saw where the glowing light was coming from.

The room was filled with skeletons—and they were alive. Or as alive as piles of dead bones could be, Eva thought. They were moving around the chamber, rattling as they walked. An eerie glow shone from their yellowing bones.

Sitting in the center of them was Hector. Her brother looked frozen in fear. The skeletons were circling him as though he were some kind of prize.

I've got to get him out of there, Eva thought. *But how?*

Before she could make a plan, one of the skeletons began to speak. Its jawbones moved up and down, and a shaky voice creaked out.

"Where isss the sssilver ssskull, boy?" the skeleton asked. "We thought you had it."

"I don't know what you're talking about," Hector said, his voice shaking.

The skeleton leaned over, its skull hovering inches above Hector's face.

"We know you are aware of the sssskull," it said. "It doesss not really belong to you. It isss oursss. You will help usss get it. We can't sssteal your life forssss without it."

Hector's face turned pale. "My life force?"

The skeletons all chuckled at once, filling the chamber with dusty laughs.

"It isss our revenge, boy," the skeleton said. "We are the sssspiritsss of the forgotten ansssses-torsss. Every Day of the Dead, other ssssspiritsss are left ofrendasss of food and drink and flow-erssss. But for yearsss and yearssss, no one hasss remembered usss. We have no comfort in the world of the dead. But with your life forssss, we can return to the living."

Eva's skin prickled as she heard the skeleton's words. In one of the books her Tia Rosa had sent, she had read that the ancestor spirits could become unhappy or angry if *ofrendas* were not made. That must be what happened to these spirits. And if they wanted Hector's life force, that could only mean . . .

"Hector!" Eva cried out without thinking.

The skeletons all turned at once, fixing their hollow eyes on Eva. Before she could run, two of the skeletons grabbed her by the arms. Their bony fingers felt cold and sharp against her skin.

"Let me go!" Eva cried. Then she had an idea. "I know where the skull is, not Hector. Let us go and I'll bring it to you."

The lead skeleton tapped its chin bone with a long, thin finger. "You may be telling the truth," it said. "And you may not. We will keep the boy until you return."

"Eva, don't bring it to them!" Hector cried.

Eva gave Hector a look that she hoped he would understand. The look said, *Don't worry, I'm going to think of something*.

Then she turned to the lead skeleton and took a deep breath. "Deal," she said. "Now tell these guys to let go."

The lead skeleton nodded, and the skeletons loosened their grips on Eva. She gave Hector one last look and then headed back up the dark path.

As she walked, her mind raced. If she brought the skeletons the silver skull, they might be distracted and she could help Hector escape. Then again, that might not work, and Eva would have brought the skeletons just what they wanted.

Back outside the crypt, Eva looked at the skull. She bit her lip and looked out over the cemetery, at the grave beds covered with *ofrendas*.

An idea slowly formed in her head. The skeletons were angry because they had not been left any food or flowers. Maybe if she brought them some, they'd stop being so angry. It might work— or it might just make the skeletons angrier than ever if she showed up without the skull.

If Eva brings the silver skull to the skeletons, go to page 122.

If Eva brings the skeletons *ofrendas* instead, go to page 135.

"Sorry, Abuela," Hector said. "I don't think Eva believes any of this is real. And I'm not going to that cemetery by myself, in the dark. No way."

The parrot flapped its wings. "But you must! You must!"

"We'll take it to the cemetery in the morning," Hector said, walking quickly toward the house. Eva followed him. "Won't that be okay?"

"It must be tonight!" the parrot said. It lifted off of Hector's shoulder and began to fly circles around the twins.

Hector and Eva went back into the house. Hector peeked through a curtain. The parrot was perched on a tree just outside, staring at them.

"Did you two have a nice talk?" Tia Rosa asked.

Hector spun around. "Sure," he said nervously. "Uh, is it really true that the ancestors come back in animal form? I mean really?"

Tia Rosa looked thoughtful. "Those are the stories," she said. "Whether it is true or not I cannot say. I have never talked to an ancestor in animal form before."

I have, Hector thought. *At least, I think I have.* He peeked through the window again. The parrot was gone.

Eva seemed to have returned to her old self. "Of course it's not true," she said. "That would be impossible."

Hector sighed. He cast a glance at the skull on the altar. He hoped that the talking parrot wasn't really Abuela. And he hoped Abuela was wrong about the skull.

But something inside told him she was right. He just hoped nothing bad would happen again before the morning.

Soon it was time for bed. Tia Rosa set up blankets and pillows for Hector and Eva in the living room. The adults went to bed, leaving the twins downstairs. The only light was the candles flickering on the nearby *ofrenda*.

Hector tried to sleep, but the events of the night preyed on his mind. He sat up and decided to keep an eye on the silver skull—just in case anything else happened.

His eyelids were starting to droop when Hector noticed a bright light coming from the *ofrenda*. He bolted away and saw the eyes of the silver skull glowing once again. He quickly shook Eva awake.

"It's happening again!" he whispered.

Soon the whole *ofrenda* began to shake. Hector watched as the four legs of the main table collapsed, sending the *ofrenda* crashing to the floor. The candles blew out all at once, leaving them in the dark.

There was a sound of footsteps as the adults came running downstairs. Tia Rosa switched on a light.

"What has happened?" she asked. Then she gasped when she saw the *ofrenda*.

It was worse than before. The plates of food had smashed into pieces, and the skulls and skeleton figures were crushed and broken.

"It's the silver skull!" Hector blurted out. "It's making all of the bad things happen!"

At Hector's words, a cold gust of wind filled the room. It was accompanied by a low, wailing that sounded more human than anything.

As Hector and his family watched, ghostly figures appeared in the wind. Shadows crossed their pale, angry faces. Then they spoke in one voice, a shallow whisper that made Hector shudder.

"Bad luck is in this place," the spirits said. "Bad luck that has ruined our feast. Now we are angry!"

The spirits wailed again. They began to circle the room, going faster and faster each time. Pillows flew off the couch. Glasses fell from their cabinets. Paintings fell from the wall. Books jumped off their shelves.

The door flew open by itself, and the parrot flew inside.

"You should have listened to me, my children!" squawked Abuela. "You should have listened to me!"

THE END

Continued from page 140

Eva climbed back into bed. "Go to sleep, Hector. It's the best thing to do," she said.

Hector got in bed and pulled the covers over his ears. He could still hear the music. But he was tired, and he felt his eyes droop.

Then, he wasn't sure how, he found himself opening up the front door and walking out into the street. He could sense Eva behind him. The sound of the music was louder now, calling to him.

It's another dream, Hector thought. His mind felt hazy and unclear. But he could feel the grit beneath his bare feet as he walked down the street. He could smell the spicy scent of food cooking through the windows in the nearby houses. Slowly, he began to realize he wasn't dreaming. This was real. But he could not stop following the music.

Eva walked silently by his side, her eyes wide. They walked and walked, turning as the music grew louder and louder.

And then they saw it. The ghost stood at the end of the street. He held out a skinny arm, beckoning toward them. Hector cringed at the sight of his evil-looking face, but he could not turn away.

It was as though the music had a hold of him, somehow.

The twins stopped just inches in front of the ghost. A sick, rotting smell floated toward Hector's nostrils. He coughed.

The ghost pointed at Hector. He looked down at his own left hand. He hadn't realized it before, but he was gripping the *calaca* of the mariachis that he and Eva had given to Tia Rosa.

The ghost held open his palm. Bones peeked out through rotting flesh. Hector placed the *calaca* in the ghost's palm. He shivered as his fingers made contact with the creature.

"This belongs to me," the ghost said in a low and raspy voice. "You have taken what is mine. Now you will pay."

"We didn't take it!" Eva cried out. "We bought it! In a store!"

The ghost ignored her. Hector willed his feet to run, but they wouldn't move. The ghost had some kind of hold over them.

Hector watched as the ghost placed the *calaca* on the ground. Then he pointed his finger at it. Sparks flew from his fingertips, striking the *calaca*.

In the space of an instant, the *calaca* grew, until two life-sized skeletons were standing before Hector and Eva. They did not look like they were made of papier-mâché. They looked real.

And then they moved. The guitar player tuned the strings on his guitar. The other mariachi gave his maracas a shake.

"Play, my friends!" said the ghost. "Play, and let us watch these thieves dance!"

"We're not thieves!" Hector protested, but his voice was drowned out by the sound of the mariachi players. As soon as the music started, Hector felt his feet begin to move on their own.

He looked over at Eva. She was dancing, too. She looked like some kind of puppet being pulled by invisible strings.

"I can't stop!" Eva shouted over the music.

"Me, neither!" Hector shouted back.

The ghost laughed. "Dance! Dance until you become a ghost like me!"

Hector felt panic well up inside him. He couldn't really make them dance forever, could he?

The ghost grinned. "Yes I can!" he said as though he had read Hector's mind. "Yes I can!"

THE END

Continued from page 114

Eva didn't want to risk making the skeletons angry. She picked up the skull. It was small—only about the size of her fist—but it was solid and heavy. An idea formed in her mind.

Eva gripped the skull tightly and made her way back into the dark crypt. She followed the path down to the chamber. The skeletons were standing in front of Hector, with the lead skeleton in front.

"Do you have the ssskull, girl?" the skeleton asked.

Eva held it up. "Here it is," she said. "Catch!"

And then Eva hurled the silver skull as hard and fast as she could, aimed right at the lead skeleton's own bony skull. There was a sickening sound as the skull shattered into pieces that flew all over the chamber. A strangled cry came from somewhere deep inside the lead skeleton. Then its bones collapsed to the floor with a clatter.

The other skeletons stood still, as though they were in shock. Eva knew they didn't have much time. The silver skull rolled to her brother's feet.

"Hector, pick it up!" she cried.

Hector picked up the skull and ran to Eva's side. The other skeletons charged at them, crying in fury. Eva noticed another passageway just to their left. She grabbed Hector by the arm and led them through it.

"We can't let them get the silver skull," Eva said as they ran.

"I know," Hector said. "Once they were done with me, they were going to try to steal the life forces of everyone in the cemetery."

"Let's just hope this path leads us out of here!" Eva said.

Eva tried not to look back. Behind them, she could hear the sound of rattling bones as the skeletons chased after them.

As her eyes adjusted to the darkness, Eva thought she saw some kind of opening up ahead. As they got closer, she saw it was the back of another crypt. She and Hector climbed inside. Eva looked around for something to block the entrance with.

She didn't have to look hard. A stone slab large enough to cover the hole had been pushed right to the side of the entrance. She and Hector each grabbed an end and pushed as hard as they could.

They were a few inches away from closing the door when a skeletal hand reached through the crack, grabbing a lock of Eva's hair. She screamed.

"Hector! Help!"

Hector smacked the bony hand until it retreated.

Then he and Eva pushed one last time.

The entrance was closed. On the other side, the skeletons scratched at it with their pointy fingers.

"Thank goodness," Eva said, breathing a sigh of relief. "Now we can go out the front."

The twins turned around. The crypt held two empty coffins, one on either of the side walls. On the opposite wall they saw a stone door.

Eva ran to it and pushed.

Nothing happened.

Hector joined her. They pushed and pulled. The front door of the crypt was closed tightly.

Behind them, the scratching sound of the skeletons grew louder.

Hector began pounding on the door. "Help!" he screamed. "Help! We're in here!"

Eva joined him, pounding and screaming.

"Don't worry," Eva said finally. "Someone will hear us soon. Someone will come and find us."

"Before the skeletons do?" Hector asked.

"Sure," Eva said. But deep down, she wasn't sure.

Not sure at all.

THE END

"Let's try the first one you said," Hector suggested. "If it doesn't work, we can always try the other one."

Eva nodded her head. "Okay. On the count of three. One, two, three."

The twins said the words together out loud. *"Mas malo mas. Mas malo mas. Mas malo mas. Mas malo mas. Mas malo mas. Mas malo mas. Mas malo mas."*

When they were finished, the green light died in the skull's eyes. An invisible wind swept away the cold mist.

"We did it!" Hector said. "You were right the first time."

"I guess I was," Eva said.

"So what now?" Hector asked.

"Let's go home," Eva said. "I think we should leave the skull here. You'll probably just start imagining new things that it's doing."

"It wasn't my imagination!" Hector protested. "How can you say that after all of this?"

"I'm just glad it's over," Eva said. "Let's get out of here."

But before they could take a step, the ground began to shake again. This time, the force of the moving earth sent Hector and Eva flying backward. Hector landed on his back, inches away from the hard, stone slab.

"Eva!" Hector cried out. He sat up, trying to catch his breath. The fall had knocked the wind out of him.

Hector saw his sister sprawled on a grave bed a few feet away. Her eyes were open, but she looked dazed.

Hector scrambled to his feet. He started to run forward, but the ground beneath him moved again, and he fell facedown into the grass.

Hector lifted up his head. Eva was sitting up on the grave bed now, looking more alert.

Then Hector saw something rise up behind her. It looked like a hand. A white, bony hand.

Like the hand of a skeleton.

"Eva, look out!" Hector screamed.

Eva looked behind her and let out a shriek. She jumped to her feet, but the skeleton hand grabbed her by the ankle, and she fell down once again.

Hector ran to her side and pulled her up. She kicked out of the skeleton's grip and jumped off the grave bed.

"What's happening?" she yelled.

Hector was too stunned to answer. All around them, skeletons were pushing their way through the earth, climbing out of their grave beds. Moss and worms clung to their yellowing, bony bodies.

"Let's get out of here!" Hector screamed.

They started to run. The skeletons leapt off their grave beds, their bones rattling as they moved. They shot after Hector and Eva, reaching out with their long, thin arms.

The twins ran to the cemetery gate, but three skeletons stood there, grinning widely. Hector and Eva spun around. What looked like an army of skeletons was coming toward them.

"I guess maybe we didn't say the right words," Hector said.

"No," Eva said. "I guess we didn't."

THE END

Eva looked at the skull's glowing eyes and knew in her own bones that Hector was right—there was something weird about the skull.

That's the difference between me and Hector, Eva thought. *Hector hides when something weird happens. But I want to find out what it is.*

"All right, skull," Eva said out loud. "What do you want?"

The skull suddenly grew hot in Eva's hand. She dropped it onto the stone grave and took a step back.

Rainbow-colored light beams shot out of the skull's eyes, like something from a laser show, and began sweeping across the sky. A hush came over the cemetery and Eva realized that everyone was staring up, looking at the lights.

Then the rainbow colors began to swirl together, and then they changed again until the sky was lit up with a fine mist of shimmering color. Everyone gathered together to watch what would happen next.

Eva stood, transfixed by the lights, and unsure of what to do. If the skull was evil, like Hector said, then something really bad must be happening. But Eva didn't get that feeling at all. She decided to wait and see what happened next.

As the crowd watched, figures appeared in the droplets of mist. At first, they looked like blobs, but they slowly grew to look more and more human. Eva watched, open-mouthed, as the sky became filled with transparent men, women, and children.

"Mama!" someone in the crowd cried out.

"Maria!"

"Alejandro!"

As more and more names were cried out, Eva realized what she was seeing. Somehow, the skull was making the spirits of the ancestors visible for everyone to see.

Through the noise, she heard Tia Rosa's voice. "Sister!"

Eva slowly walked to her aunt, who had her arms outstretched toward one of the figures in the sky. Eva saw a round, smiling woman with curly hair like Tia Rosa's.

Eva's parents had their arms around Tia Rosa, and Eva could see they were all crying. Eva walked over and squeezed her mother's hand.

"It's your abuela," Mrs. Ramirez breathed.

Eva looked up at the smiling face, a face she hadn't seen since she was a baby. Her grandmother put her fingers to her lips and blew Eva a kiss.

Then the figures began to slowly fade away.

Seconds later, the shimmering rainbow mist was gone, and the sky was once again black, marked only with stars.

Eva watched the adults' faces change, as though they were waking from a dream. Eva's mother turned to Tia Rosa.

"Was that real?" she asked.

"It is the Day of the Dead," Tia Rosa said. "Anything can happen."

The cemetery became filled with the sound of soft whispers as people discussed what had just happened. Eva walked back to the crypt and picked up the skull.

"Thank you," she said. "I know Tia Rosa will give you a good home."

Eva looked up at the sky.

Poor Hector, she thought. *He never should have stayed home!*

THE END

Continued from page 108

Hector thought about it. "Doesn't *malo* mean bad or evil in Spanish?" he asked. "And *mas* means more. So maybe it's *malo no mas*. Evil no more. Right?"

Eva made a face that told Hector she wished she had thought of that first.

"*Malo no mas*," she said. "Just like I said. So let's say it seven times."

The twins counted down to three, then repeated the words Abuela had told them to say. "*Malo no mas. Malo no mas. Malo no mas. Malo no mas. Malo no mas. Malo no mas. Malo no mas.*"

The mist around them began to swirl in circles, circles that whipped faster and faster, until Hector and Eva felt like they were in the center of a hurricane. Eva's dark hair whipped around her face.

"Maybe I was wrong!" Hector shouted over the wind.

Then, as suddenly as it had sprung up, the swirling mist vanished. The cemetery was as quiet and still as when they had first arrived.

Hector looked down at the silver skull.

It was gone.

"I think we were right," Eva said. "I think we did it!"

"Me, too," Hector said. "Now let's get out of here."

Walking back past the grave beds, Hector noticed that the cemetery did not feel as spooky as it had before. He looked up at the trees, hoping to see the parrot. Maybe now that the skull was gone, Abuela's spirit could return to visit them. The tree leaves blew slightly in the breeze, but there was no sign of the parrot.

The twins walked home and quietly entered Tia Rosa's house. The candles still flickered on the *ofrenda*, and Hector thought how beautiful and peaceful it looked. He stared at the dancing flames until he fell asleep.

The next morning, Tia Rosa was already awake, stirring up a new batch of filling for the tamales. She was in a cheerful mood, singing as she worked. Hector and Eva got into the spirit of things, and by lunchtime, all of the tamales were finished. Hector wanted to eat one right away, but Tia Rosa told them they had to wait until they went to the cemetery that night.

Tia Rosa did not even ask about the missing skull, and Hector was glad. Without the skull in the house, everything seemed lighter, happier. After the tamales, they helped Tia Rosa make empanadas, little pastries stuffed with meat and fried until they were golden-brown. Hector's stomach rumbled at the delicious smells. They piled the finished food onto the *ofrenda*.

Tia Rosa wrapped her arms around the twins. "Abuela would be so happy to see you here," she said, smiling.

Hector and Eva looked at each other and smiled, too.

When the sun went down, everyone in the family grabbed a plate from the *ofrenda* and they walked to the cemetery. Hector marveled at how different the cemetery looked from the night before. The grave beds were covered with red and orange flowers, glowing candles, and plates of food. Families gathered around the graves, talking quietly or singing.

Tia Rosa led them to Abuela's grave and they decorated it with everything they had brought from the *ofrenda*. When they were done, Tia Rosa and Hector's parents shared more stories about Abuela. Then Tia Rosa picked up the platters of tamales and empanadas.

"We will share with our neighbors," she said. "Tonight, everyone feasts."

Soon the families around them were passing around plates of tamales, empanadas, pastries, chocolate, and bread. Hector and Eva each filled a plate and began to happily eat, facing Abuela's picture.

Then Hector heard Tia Rosa exclaim behind them. "Look at that! A parrot!"

A colorful bird swooped down and landed right next to Abuela's picture.

"Good children!" squawked the parrot. "Did it right! Did it right!"

"Isn't that unusual," Tia Rosa said. "It's as though the parrot is talking to Hector and Eva."

The parrot winked at the twins. Then it flew away, disappearing into the darkness.

"Thanks, Abuela," Hector whispered. "It was nice meeting you!"

THE END

Continued from page 114

Eva ran back to Abuela's grave. Tia Rosa and her parents were over at a nearby grave, talking to a family there. Eva thought about asking them for help. But by the time she'd explain what had happened—and who would believe her?—it might be too late to save Hector.

She knelt down in front of Abuela's picture. "I'm sorry, Abuela," she said. "I hope you don't mind if I take some of your *ofrendas*. Hector needs them."

Looking at her grandmother's smiling face, Eva was sure that she wouldn't mind at all. She took a plate of oranges and piled on some apples, tamales, empanadas, and marigold flowers—as much as the plate could hold. Then she ran back to the crypt.

Eva carefully made her way back down the steep path to the chamber. The skeletons had gathered closer around Hector. Her brother's face had a brave look, but Eva knew he was terrified.

"Did you bring me the ssskull, girl?" the lead skeleton asked.

"No," Eva said. She carefully placed the plate at the skeleton's feet. "I brought you something else. *Ofrendas*."

"Foolisssh girl! I need the sssskull!" the skeleton cried.

Eva took a step back. She had done the wrong thing.

The skeleton lifted a leg and moved to kick the plate. Then it stopped.

Eva held her breath. There was a creaking sound as the skeleton squatted down to get closer to the plate.

"Tamalesss," it said finally. "Jusssst like my abuela usssed to make."

The skeleton picked up a tamale in one of its bony hands. It crunched on the tamale with its rotting teeth. A piece of tamale bounced down its neck-bone and got stuck in its rib cage.

But the skeleton seemed happy. It beckoned to the other skeletons.

"Come, my friendsss!" it cried. "Let usss eat!"

The skeletons surrounded Eva and Hector and the plate of *ofrendas*. They grabbed oranges and apples. One skeleton picked up a marigold flower and stuck it in its skull where its left ear would have been. Soon the floor of the chamber was littered with chomped and broken pieces of tamales, empanadas, apples, and oranges.

Finally, the plate was empty. The skeleton looked at Hector and Eva.

"Thank you," it said. "We have waited sssso

long for our *ofrendassss*. Now we can ressst in
peasssse for the resssst of the year."

"We will tell Tia Rosa about you," Eva said.
"We will make sure she leaves *ofrendas* for you
every year."

The skeleton nodded. Then it turned and
began to walk down a nearby passageway. The
other skeletons got in line and followed it out.

"Come on, Hec," Eva said. "Let's get out of
here."

Eva and Hector climbed back up the steep
passage.

"Do you think Tia Rosa will believe us?"
Hector asked.

They reached the entrance of the crypt. Eva
could see Tia Rosa standing right outside, smiling
at them. She was holding the silver skull.

"I think she will," Eva said. "I think she will."

THE END

Continued from page 46

Hector and Eva ran into the nearby alley. It let out into the street right next to it. They ran up the street, turned the corner, and headed back to Tia Rosa's house.

Hector didn't look behind him until they reached Tia Rosa's steps. There was no sign of the ghost—if that's what it was—anywhere. Hector let out a deep breath.

The twins were both sweaty and dirty, but exhausted, so they climbed into bed and fell right to sleep. The next morning, they were awakened by sun streaming through the windows and a delicious smell from the kitchen. Hector and Eva looked at each other.

"We must have been dreaming," Eva said as though she knew what Hector was going to ask. Hector just nodded. He hoped it had been a dream. The memory of that ghost's horrible face was too terrible to be real.

After a breakfast of eggs and peppers and tortillas, they helped Tia Rosa get ready for the Day of the Dead. She showed them how to spoon meat filling into corn husks and fold the husks into little packets to make tamales. She took them all into town to buy sugar skulls. Eva wanted to take hers home, but Hector took a bite out of his right away. It was the sweetest thing he had ever tasted. They went to a bakery and bought a loaf of bread shaped like a skull for the *ofrenda*, too.

They piled everything on the *ofrenda* during the day, and when the sun went down, they took everything to the cemetery a few blocks away. The grave sites were lit by bright candles and surrounded by families quietly talking. Hector and Eva's family piled everything on the grave of their abuela, and after an hour or so, they began to share the food with their neighbors. Soon everyone was feasting.

Hector never once felt scared or creepy in the cemetery. Everyone seemed to be happy, talking and remembering their family members. And all of the food was delicious. When he finally climbed into bed late that night, he felt happy and full.

Hector woke in the middle of the night to the sound of music. He sat up. It was the same sound as the night before, the same sound he had heard in Bleaktown. Once again, Eva was awake, too. Hector was tempted to follow the sound to the front door. But the memory of the scary-looking ghost stopped him.

"We can't listen to it," he said. "Maybe we should wake up Mom and Dad."

"Or Tia Rosa," Eva said. "I have a feeling she

will know what to do."

Eva started to walk up the stairs. Then she stopped.

"This is silly," she said. "It's just music. Let's just go back to sleep and ignore it."

Hector frowned. There was something about the music that, well, didn't want to be ignored.

If the twins tell Tia Rosa about the music, go to page 78.

If the twins go back to sleep, go to page 119.

"Let's try Tia Rosa's first," Hector said. It felt good, standing up to Eva again. "That's easier, right?"

"All right," Eva relented.

The two walked down the side street and made their way back to Tia Rosa's house. Hector carried the skull, and Eva had the list of ingredients Señor Grito gave them.

"It won't be long now," Hector told the skull. "We'll be rid of you for good!"

At Hector's words, the skull's eyes began to glow a pale green.

"Uh-oh," Hector said.

A fast, cold wind suddenly whipped up around them. Hector heard Eva scream beside him. He looked to see the list of ingredients fly out of her hand!

"No!" Hector cried.

Eva and Hector ran after the flying paper. But the wind carried it up, up, above the trees, until it vanished from their sight.

"We've got to go back to the shop," Eva said. Hector nodded. They ran as fast as they could until they reached the narrow side street.

But when they came to Señor Grito's shop,

they found that the front door was boarded up with wood; the windows were empty and revealed a shop filled with dust, cobwebs—and nothing else.

"This can't be right," Hector said. "Maybe it's the wrong store."

The twins ran up and down the street, but they could not find Señor Grito's shop. They tried other streets, wandering through the neighborhood until their feet hurt. Finally, Hector sank down to the curb.

"You know what this means?" he asked Eva.

His sister nodded. "Without Señor Grito's list, we can't make the potion. And without the potion . . ."

"We'll have bad luck forever!" Hector wailed.

THE END

Hector and Eva's family flew back home the next morning. Hector felt a little sad leaving. Tia Rosa was so nice, and despite the scary skeletons, he had really liked experiencing the Day of the Dead. He hadn't missed trick-or-treating at all.

By the time they got back from the airport, it was already the afternoon. Hector didn't wait to unpack. He wanted to get rid of the silver skull as soon as possible.

He stuck his head in Eva's room. "Come on," he said. "I want to get rid of this thing!"

Eva nodded, and they headed out to Wary Lane. Hector was glad to see that the strange shop was open. They entered and walked up to the counter. Mr. Cream was sitting on his stool, reading an old book with a leather cover.

He smiled when he saw them. "How was your Day of the Dead?" he asked.

Hector placed the skull on the table. "It was good. Until the part when skeletons came to life and wanted to use the silver skull to steal my life force."

Mr. Cream chuckled. "Well, I see they didn't succeed."

Hector was startled by his response. But he

143

guessed Mr. Cream was right. Everything had turned out fine.

"We want our money back," Eva said boldly. "You know, you shouldn't be selling things like this in your store. Something really bad could happen."

Mr. Cream's emerald eyes twinkled. "If my customers make the right choices, there will always be a happy ending," he said mysteriously.

Then he reached into his cash register, took out some bills, and handed them to Hector.

"Thank you for your business," he said.

"Okay then," Hector said.

At that moment, the bell on the front door tinkled. A strange-looking boy marched up to the counter. He had dark hair and very thick glasses in dark frames.

"Excuse me," he asked Mr. Cream, completely ignoring Hector and Eva. "Do you sell old comic books here?"

Hector and Eva walked out of the store.

"I guess Mr. Cream was right," Hector said. "Everything turned out fine."

Eva frowned. "I still think he shouldn't be selling things like that skull," she said, casting a suspicious glance at the door.

THE END